ICE LORD INCOGNITO

MONSTERS, PI, BOOK 2

AVA ROSS

ENCHANTED STAR PRESS

ICE LORD INCOGNITO

Monsters, PI, Book 2

Covers by EDH Professionals

Editing: JA Wren and Owl Eyes Proofs & Edits

No AI was used to write this book or make the covers in this series.

For my readers.
I couldn't do this without you!

ALSO BY AVA ROSS

You can find Ava's books on Amazon

& on her website, avarosswrites(dot)com.

ICE LORD INCOGNITO

Will true love thaw the heart of Ice Lord Incognito?

Melly: When my grandmother is arrested for poisoning the members of her social club, I hire Monsters, PI to help clear her name. My case is assigned to an ice lord, Elrik, the guy I met a week ago at a wedding and haven't been able to stop thinking about. As we track down clues and discover there's a lot more going on at Grannie's social club than potluck suppers, I start hoping I can thaw this ice lord's heart. But he was recently burned, and he's not sure if he's ready to try again. Can I convince Elrik to give love another chance?

Elrik: After the woman I thought I loved cheated on me with my brother, I swore off relationships for good. I planned to settle in Mystic Harbor and focus on my new job as an investigator at Monsters, PI. No relationships. No falling in love. But my vow is tested when I meet

Melly. She's cute and funny, and I ache to back her against a wall and kiss her.

After I clear her grandmother's name, do I dare claim Melly as an ice lord's bride?

Ice Lord Incognito is Book 2 in the Monsters, PI Series. It's a cute and steamy romance featuring a cinnamon roll ice lord, on-the-page heat, a cozy mystery, humor, and a HEA guaranteed.

Other Books in the Series:
Undercover Orc (a companion story in Sweet Monster Treats)
Secret Agent Gargoyle
Ice Lord Incognito
Dragon Detective
Top Secret Vampire
Ogre on Patrol

1

MELLY

It isn't often that a woman has to make bail for her eighty-year-old grandmother after she's arrested for poisoning the fellow members of her church social club. Grannie Rose was tough and serious, but one of the most caring people I knew. There was no way she'd poison her friends. She stuck to her values no matter what and would never lie or break the law. I should know. She'd raised me from the time I was twelve, doing all she could to instill in me her strict moral code and deep respect for doing what was right.

Yet, here I was, bringing her home from the county jail. At least they didn't fingerprint her while she was there.

Pulling into the driveway of her modest ranch home, I brought my car to a halt and shut off the engine.

"I'm grateful your seats have heaters," she said, tucking her shawl around her throat. "It was rather cold in that cell. I'll be lodging a formal complaint with the mayor. You can help me with that."

"Of course."

"My shawl was *not* enough. I should've thought to wear a coat, but it's May, for heaven's sake. Who needs a coat in Cape Cod in May?"

When she called me, I thought it was a joke, one of those pranks where someone pays to have a person arrested to benefit a charity. But, nope, my Grannie Rose had been arrested for poisoning six of her fellow social club members. One of them was still in the hospital, and the DA was thinking about pressing charges.

She hadn't done it. Nothing would convince me she had.

"Who do you think is out to get you?" I asked.

"I'm not sure." Grannie Rose blinked my way. "It could be just about anyone."

"Who was there when you made your punch?" Her secret punch was as renowned in this small town of Mystic Harbor as her knitting. Her handcrafted mittens sold within seconds at local craft fairs each fall, and she'd won the Good Citizen Award for her mitten donations three years in a row.

"I was alone when I made it." She frowned. "You know how it is. I don't share my recipe with anyone." She patted my arm. "Except my beloved granddaughter, Melly, naturally."

I'd insisted on the nickname when I moved in with my grandmother after my mother died. My dad had taken off not long after I was born, and he'd died before Mom. Melly fit. New life, new name. From that moment on, I'd left Melinda behind and became an entirely new person, or so I'd thought when I was twelve.

Grannie, of course, had no problem calling me Melly. She hated her real name of Rosebud, and who wouldn't?

I got out of the car and went around to her side, removing her walker from the back seat before opening her door.

After she fell at the church function hall and broke her hip a few months ago, I'd moved into the small apartment on top of her gambrel garage. I wanted to be here to help her after she came home from rehab. In exchange for driving, housework, and preparing most of her meals, she gave me a great deal on the building she owned on Main Street for Creature Cones, the ice cream shop I'd opened two months ago.

I helped her get out of the car and stand, supporting her until her hands tightly gripped her walker. I shut the door and followed as she rounded the hood of my car and started up the walk toward her back kitchen door.

"Tell me what happened. You made the punch," I prompted. "There had to be others around because I know you'd never poison anyone."

"Thank you," she gushed, grinning up at me.

At five-feet-tall, she was as petite as a pixie. At five-eleven, I was as tall as a . . . well, a Valkyrie, I suppose. I loved my height and often wore boots with heels to add to it. I just needed a sword and a fur outfit to complete my Valkyrie image.

"I appreciate your support," she said as she reached the top of the ramp leading to her side entrance. I unlocked the door, and we entered the kitchen. "Detective Carter was quite insistent that I'd done the crime, and I would need to do the time."

"You're not going to jail," I growled.

"I agree." She moved across the kitchen and settled in a chair at the small table. "What's the game plan, dear?"

"As soon as you're settled, I'm calling Monsters, PI."

2

ELRIK

"I'm assigning this new case to you," my orc boss and owner of Monsters, PI, Katar Dolkin, said. He'd just entered my office and taken the seat across from my desk.

In his past job, Katar did extensive undercover work. But while recently solving a case involving an ancient orc manuscript stolen from the local library, he'd fallen in love with the librarian, Bailey. Rather than return to the orc kingdom, he'd opted to remain in town, marry her, and set up a new business. He'd hired me, and I'd started working at Monsters, PI, a few weeks ago.

Not long ago, monsters stepped forward, joining human society. Finding welcome among them, we formed treaties with their governments. Now that many of us had settled in various towns across the globe, it was common to see centaurs working at the gas station, demons running businesses, and monsters of all varieties dating and marrying humans. Despite the horror stories humans had grown up with that featured monsters as the villain, they'd been surprisingly eager to be with us. Monster romance novels had led the way.

Eager to get away from the area I'd grown up in, I'd recently moved to town and taken a job with Katar. I'd solved one case already, and I was eager to take on another.

"Our newest client will be here in a few moments to explain." Katar's serious gaze met mine. "Melly's an old friend of Bailey's. They went to school together. You might remember her from Angie and Tuvid's wedding. She was one of Angie's bridesmaids."

Tuvid was a gargoyle and also employed at Monsters, PI. While solving Angie's missing beer keg case, they'd fallen in love. I'd attended their wedding a week ago. Tuvid and Angie had left for their honeymoon immediately after the wedding and wouldn't be back in town for a few more days. That left me, Katar, and our newest employee, a dragon shifter detective who wouldn't start until next week, to cover any cases that came in. A vampire was coming in for an interview soon, as was an ogre, and I couldn't wait to meet them and see if they'd fit in with the team.

As for Melly . . . Yeah, I remembered her. Tall, she had legs that went on forever. Greenish-brown eyes. Long dark hair I'd wanted to wrap around my hand until I could tug her against me. I'd lift her delicate chin and—

"Ah, you do remember Melly," Katar said with a low laugh. His eyes gleamed, but he couldn't know that I hadn't been able to get that woman out of my mind since I met her.

"Yes, I do," I said.

When we met, I'd messed things up. Instead of speaking with her like I'd wanted to, I froze, a total cliché for an ice lord. I'd muttered something I couldn't even recall and stumbled away from her. Me. Stumbling from someone. You wouldn't know I'd worked as a survival trainer with the military and then as a wilderness ranger and guide doing search-and-rescue for years. I was one of the most respected in my field and had regularly given interviews.

My family had been around for eons. They were distinguished. They would've sneered if they'd seen me fumble my words with anyone.

But I was attracted to Melly in a way I'd never been with anyone else.

Katar's wife, Bailey, poked her head into my office. She was covering the reception desk until we hired someone. We had a few candidates and would select one soon. "Melly's here. Should I show her in?"

"Sure." Katar rose and stalked over to his wife, stroking his knuckles across her cheek. His fingers traveled to her distended belly. Their orcling would be born soon, hence the hurry to hire more staff so Katar could take time off to be with Bailey and their young one.

Pure envy coursed through me. If only—

"I'll bring her in." Bailey curled her finger to Katar, and they kissed before she turned and strode back down the hall.

Pivoting, Katar leaned against the wall and gave me a sappy grin. They were so in love, it almost hurt to see them together.

At one time, I thought I was in love, too, but it fell apart.

Bailey returned and shot me a smile as Melly walked into the office. While Melly sat in the chair Katar had vacated, Bailey and Katar left, pulling the door closed behind them.

"Hi," Melly said, her pretty face pinkening. Why was she blushing?

"Hi." Suddenly nervous for no reason, I cleared my throat and fell back into the stiff, icy demeanor so common among my species. "I'm Elrik Nivalis," I said gruffly. "Ice lord."

She blinked. "Melly. Melly Brandt. Um, ice cream shop owner." Her sweet laugh rang out. "We met at Tuvid and Angie's wedding, which . . ." More color flooded her cheeks. "You may not remember meeting me."

"Oh, I do. You're gorgeous." Had I actually said that? It was true, but I was raised to be anything *but* spontaneous. From the time I was three, I was taught to remain in full control of my tongue and my mind.

Leave it to me to go from stumbling over my words when I first meet her to spitting almost anything out during our second meet-up.

"Thank you." She placed her phone on my desk. "I'm here for my Grannie Rose. She wants to be part of the conversation if that's okay. Since she broke her hip, she doesn't get around well, but her mind's completely clear."

"Oh, yes, sure." For an ice lord, my face felt awfully hot. Odd, since our body temperature always remained on the chilly side except when we met our—

"Thanks." She placed the call.

"Melly?" a creaky voice came through the speaker.

"Yes, Grannie. It's Melly. I'm at Monsters, PI, and I've got you on speakerphone."

"Wonderful. Who did Katar assign my case to?"

"Elrik Nivalis."

"What kind of name is Nivalis?" Grannie Rose asked, though politely.

I cleared my throat again. "I'm an ice lord. It's an ice lord name."

Grannie's cackle echoed throughout the room.

I frowned.

Melly's face pinkened even more. "I own Creature Cones, the ice cream shop on Main Street."

"I see." I didn't, but I suspected it didn't matter.

"Ice cream. Ice lord," Melly said softly.

Oh, yes.

"What does he look like?" her grandmother asked.

Melly fidgeted in her chair. "Grannie, that doesn't matter."

"It's a simple question. I've never met an ice lord, and I'm curious to know what he looks like."

"His appearance doesn't matter," Melly said stiffly. "He's been hired to solve your case."

"But it does matter. I can't be there, so you'll need to describe everything to me."

"Um, alright." Melly cringed. "His skin is blue."

"Blue like the sky or . . .?"

"Yes, like the sky. He has dark hair."

"Black? Brown? I hope it's not that dull grayish black. You know the kind."

Melly sighed. "Inky black. It's thick. Glossy. Like a night sky."

"Sounds delightful," Grannie said. "Is it cut short and proper, or does he try to look like the men on those bust-bursting romance novels we both like to read?" Grannie asked.

"Bodice rippers," Melly whispered.

Grannie grunted. "Excuse me? I didn't quite hear you."

Melly cleared her throat and lifted her voice. "They're called bodice rippers, Grannie Rose, and no, his hair isn't especially long."

I frowned. "Would you prefer I kept it longer?"

Melly's pretty hazel eyes widened. "Oh, I don't know. Maybe? It looks good like it is now, brushing your collar."

"What's his build?" Grannie asked.

"Muscular," Melly breathed, her gaze like a caress as it slid across my shoulders and chest.

My cock perked up as if it thought it was about to receive attention. I shifted in my chair and pictured glaciers. Rocky outcroppings where predators might lurk. The high-protein diet search and rescue dogs required. Anything but how pretty Melly was. How I adored her long, dark hair. How I wanted to rise from my chair and urge her up from her own. Cup her cheeks and—

My skin flashed hot again. Odd—again. If I didn't know better, I'd think she was my—

"I believe I have enough physical description to picture you now, Elrik," Grannie said. "You may proceed."

My veins simmering, I yanked on the collar of my t-shirt, pulling it away from my throat before it choked out my breath. "Very well."

"Are you single, Elrik?" her grandmother asked.

Melly winced. "Grannie."

"My granddaughter is lonely," Rose said. "She spends too much time working or sitting alone in her apartment. She needs to get out. Have fun."

Melly pinched her eyes shut and curled her shoulders forward. "I'm sorry," she whispered.

I cleared my throat, hard enough it was going to ache if I kept doing it. "I was engaged, but it's over."

"Are you on the rebar?" Grannie asked.

Melly and I frowned.

Grannie tittered. "Oh, my mistake. Rebound's the term. *Rebound*, not rebar."

"Grannie," Melly shouted. "Stop! I'm here to explain your case to Elrik. Nothing else."

"There's no harm in asking him if he'd like to attend a function with you. The church offers plenty of—"

"I'm ending the call, Grannie," Melly said sharply. "I'll tell you everything when I get home." She gouged her finger against her phone, cutting off her grandmother's protest. "I'm terribly sorry."

"I'm not. Tell me something." My voice suddenly came out fluid. Confident, for whatever reason. I leaned back in my chair. "Would you ever consider dating an ice lord?"

3

MELLY

Yes, yes, please, I wanted to shout. From the moment I met Elrik at Tuvid and Angie's wedding, he was all I could think about. I even asked Angie to give him my number, and she said she did, but when he didn't call, I assumed he wasn't interested.

"Didn't you say you just ended a relationship?" I asked. Maybe he *was* on the rebound. Everyone said rebound relationships didn't work out, and the last thing I needed to do was get tangled up in something like that.

"My ex-girlfriend is marrying my brother," he said, dragging his fingers across the back of his neck.

No wonder he hadn't called me. He was pining over the woman he loved who was marrying his brother.

He smiled, but even I could tell it was fake. "We all grew up together. I've known Brittney pretty much from the day she was born."

"Is she an ice . . . lady?"

"Yes, that's the term, and yes, her family is the same

species as mine. There aren't many of us left. From the time I was thirteen or so, I had a crush on her. We started dating about a year ago, but when I returned from my latest search-and-rescue mission, she told me she was marrying my brother."

I gulped. "Marrying?"

"Yeah," he said with a twist of his lips.

"That sucks."

He grunted. "It does. She said they fell in love. They're getting married. My heart . . ."

"Your heart what?"

"I'm going to be alright." He frowned, and while I admired his medium blue skin, he raked both of his hands across his thick black hair. His shockingly—no, icy—blue eyes met mine. "I'm doing my best to move on."

"When did you two break up?"

"Three months ago."

"I'm sorry."

"Some things work out, some don't." His fake smile rose again before quickly disappearing. "It's for the best."

He tugged on his black t-shirt that outlined all his delicious muscles. The first thing I noticed about him at the wedding was how tall he was—at least six-six. When I stood beside him, I felt petite. "But you didn't come here to talk about my relationship woes. You said you need my services?"

My breath caught. Why was I taking his words sexually?

Because I hadn't dated anyone in over a year, that was why. Even my grannie knew I was hanging around my apartment alone. Ugh.

Shaking off my mortification, I explained what happened with my grandmother.

Leaning forward, he braced his forearms on his desk. They were sinful forearms. Muscular, covered in gorgeous blue skin that *was* a bit like the sky. Nothing Smurf-like at all. "Who was there while she was making the punch?" he asked, dragging my brain back to the situation.

"She said no one. She likes to make it alone. It's a secret recipe, though I know it, of course."

"Of course." He frowned.

"I made it for the social club after Grannie fell and broke her hip. She was in the hospital and then rehab, but everyone loves her punch, so I dropped by and made it for them. She had to share the recipe, or I wouldn't have been able to do it for her."

"But you didn't make the punch this time?"

"No, she's doing better, so she took over the task again. On that evening, she insisted I drop her off at the church function room and leave. I don't attend the club meetings. It's just her and six other church members."

"I'll need their names since I'll investigate each of them." Sitting back in his chair, he frowned. "Tell me more."

"Grannie made the punch and then went to the bathroom. When she returned, everyone had arrived, and they'd started drinking the punch. She was *pissed*. She wanted to serve them, not have them dish it up themselves. She takes her punch quite seriously."

"I'm sure she does. You said everyone got sick?"

"I think so. By the time she came out of the bathroom,

some were vomiting while others had fallen and passed out on the floor. One is still hospitalized."

"Who?"

"Grannie's best friend since high school, Sue. As for the others, the hospital had to pump out a few of their stomachs. My grandmother's horrified about this. Completely distraught. She didn't do anything, but she's been accused, and Detective Carter suggested it's basically a closed case."

"Did they determine what the toxin was?"

"Xylitol."

"The sugar alcohol?" His head tilted. "Does her punch recipe include Xylitol?"

"No added sweeteners at all. Her recipe's a secret but . . ." I peered around to make sure we were alone, then leaned close to him, trying not to notice how nice he smelled. I caught the scent of apples with cinnamon, bergamot, as if he'd recently drank a cup of Earl Grey tea, and, strangely enough, a note of something akin to the lovely scent that fills the air after rain falls in the forest. "Her special ingredient is multi-colored sherbet. It gives the punch a creamy sweetness everyone adores."

"It sounds amazing. You said Sue's still in the hospital?"

"She already had kidney problems, and this isn't helping. I guess Xylitol can be toxic to the kidneys if you ingest it in large enough quantities. They're hoping there won't be lasting damage. But Grannie might go to jail for the crime." My chest was so tight, I could barely breathe. "She's eighty. She won't survive anything like that. You've got to help us." My throat was tight, and it was all I could do to get the words out. Stress made me shake. My grandmother had not done this, but how were we going to find out who did?

"I promise we'll figure this out." He pulled out a pad of paper and a pen and wrote a few things down. With his pen poised, he looked up at me through his incredibly long, black lashes, another sinful thing about this man. "Where did she buy her ingredients? Was she alone?"

"I've been purchasing everything for her. Until she broke her hip, she was getting around okay, though she's been slowing. I guess it's natural with her age. I'm happy to take her wherever she needs to go, to do things like this for her. Her Saturday night church social club is one of the few activities she insists on attending regularly. They hold a potluck dinner. Grannie always makes her secret punch. After they eat, they dance, though Grannie only sways since she's still using a walker. Then they play poker."

His thick, dark eyebrows lifted. "Poker?"

"Would you believe they play for money? In church, though the function hall is attached to the main building, not inside. For someone as straightlaced as my Grannie Rose, she's a regular card shark. She wins almost every time and often comes home with a few hundred dollars."

"She sounds like an incredible person."

I grinned. Despite her stiff demeanor, I adored my grandmother. "She really is. Everyone loves her." I leaned back in my chair. "My mother died when I was twelve, and she stepped in and finished raising me. I don't know where I'd be without her."

"You don't have any other family?"

"It's just us. I had no siblings, and my dad took off before I was born. He died before Mom. I've got a few aunts and uncles, but they live on the other side of the country and never visit. Other than one stepcousin—"

He looked up from his paper. "Stepcousin?"

"Ginny. She's a few years older than me. Her dad married Grannie's sister, but the marriage ended before Ginny got used to calling my grandmother Auntie Rose."

"Where are Ginny and her father now?"

"Her dad's dead, and Ginny lives here in Mystic Harbor. She's a caregiver for a man who's mostly homebound."

He nodded slowly and made a few more notes. "Would any of your distant relatives benefit from harming you or your grandmother?"

"I doubt it. When I say they never visit, what I mean is that they don't write or call or even send a Christmas card. We have no communication with them at all."

"Why not?"

I shrugged. "Grannie only had one child, my mother, and Dad's relatives have busy lives. They weren't interested in being a part of mine, so we've basically lost touch."

"If you can give me their names and where they live, I'll check them out before crossing them off the list."

"I doubt they're involved. Grannie is comfortable, but she's not wealthy. Her only big asset is a building on Main Street with a few storefronts. I rent one for Creature Cones. She owns her home, but it's a small ranch. I live in the apartment above the garage. When she was discharged, the rehab center said she'd need help for a while, though the physical therapist who comes in twice a week said she'll be able to get around without the walker soon. Since I want to keep Grannie in her home as long as possible, I moved into the apartment. I plan to remain there indefinitely."

"That's admirable."

"She raised me. It's my turn to help her."

"Give me the names of those who attend the social club, and I'll start looking into this."

I listed them off. "I'd like to be involved in the case if I can. I'm sure I'll be able to add insight."

"I usually work alone."

"Can you make an exception in this case?"

He gave me a long look before laying his pen on the paper. "Alright. We'll handle it together."

4

ELRIK

Why was I so eager to include Melly in this investigation? As I told her, I always worked alone. I wasn't eager to take on a sidekick in a case like this. And I hadn't even asked Katar if such a thing was allowed.

But this case shouldn't be dangerous. We were talking about someone slipping Xylitol into a punchbowl, not arsenic. Someone probably did it as a prank, not realizing the substance could be toxic to someone with kidney disease. They'd come forward soon and confess, and we'd close the case. There was no reason I couldn't take some time during the investigation to get to know her better.

Despite telling myself I wasn't going to get involved with anyone else again, I liked her. She was gorgeous. Extra curvy—just the way I liked a woman. I couldn't decide if her eyes were green, gray, or brown, and I wanted to stare into them for hours until I decided. It was all I could do not to get out of my chair, round my desk, and tug her up to face me. I'd run my fingers through her dark hair gleaming in the muted light, stroke her cheeks, and tease the pad of my thumb across the tiny dimple in her chin.

Kiss her.

Hold on. I couldn't kiss her. I'd promise myself I wasn't going to date anyone, be with anyone, or kiss anyone for a while. It had only been a few months since Brittney ditched me for my brother. Rebound relationships never worked out.

Yet here I was . . .

I hadn't made a true vow not to go out with anyone. It was a mental suggestion, one that my heart and body were rebelling against already.

For now, I needed to focus on this investigation.

"I'd like to speak with your grandmother about this," I said.

Melly lifted her phone. "Do you want me to call her again?"

"In person might work best. Do you think she'd be willing to talk to me now?"

"I'm sure she would." Melly stood. "Do you want to ride with me or follow my car?"

"I'll ride with you if you can bring me back here afterward."

"I can do that."

We exited the building and crossed the street to the public parking lot on the opposite side and climbed into her car.

"Tight fit," she said, shooting me a smile as she buckled. "Sorry."

"I'm used to it. Once I moved to town, I bought a

pickup truck." Slouching lower to keep my head from grinding against the roof of her car, I buckled as well.

"All the monsters in the area drive them." She started the vehicle and backed out of her spot, taking us out onto Main Street and through the downtown area.

"Many of the vehicle manufacturers have come out with new lines built specifically for monsters."

"I don't believe I've ever ridden in a truck," she said.

I flashed her a smile. "I'll be happy to take you out in mine whenever you'd like."

"Can we go off-roading and splash through mud?"

My laugh burst out. "You just want to get my truck dirty."

She winked my way. "I do love getting dirty."

5

MELLY

I was flirting with someone I'd just hired, and I loved it. But . . . He was on the rebound from a bad breakup, and I could tell he'd been hurt. He wouldn't feel ready to try with someone new.

At my comment, he stilled in his seat, staring out the windshield. "How dirty are we talking about?"

Should I take this farther?

I hadn't dated in over two years, and my most recent attempt was a Tinder dude who catfished me. My last intimate moment was with the monster toy in my bedside table and even that had been a while. I liked Elrik; I hadn't been able to stop thinking about him after we met. I'd stared at him during Tuvid and Angie's wedding to the point one of the other bridesmaids told me to speak with him. Which I did. He muttered something and disappeared.

Silly me had pictured Elrik and I standing at the altar instead of our friends, a dream that had bordered on creepy. I'd thought I'd long since ditched fanciful dreams, that I'd left them in my past, where they belonged.

If I let that hold me back, I'd never know if we stood a chance, right?

My heart nodded, so I went for it.

"As dirty as you'd like it to be," I said, my voice all breathy. Tightening my grip on the steering wheel, I waited to hear what he'd say. I had to release my grip on the wheel to turn the corner, taking my car down the road I lived on with Grannie.

He didn't say anything, and while I'd like to call the silence companionable, tension thrived in the air.

"I shouldn't have said that," I finally said.

"It's okay." He flashed me a smile that didn't reach his eyes.

"I'm sorry." Maybe my comment reminded him of his ex. He'd pretty much said he was in love with her. And now she was marrying his brother. "Wouldn't you just like to kick other people sometimes?"

His laugh snorted out. "Yes, I would."

I wanted to ask if he still loved her or if he'd started to get over the pain, but I wasn't sure I wanted to hear his answer. By the time I'd pulled into the driveway, put the vehicle in park, and shut off the engine, my heart was beginning to accept that nothing would come of this.

All thoughts of flirting with him or pushing to see if he was open to someone new had flown away. "I'll keep this professional. I promise."

He unbuckled and turned in his seat to face me. When he cupped my cheeks with his surprisingly chilly hands, I released a shiver. "You're lovely. I don't believe I've ever met anyone as special as you."

Now he'd add "but".

"I want to kiss you," he said instead.

"Then why don't you?" I croaked.

"It's forbidden."

That, I hadn't expected. "Forbidden by who?"

His hands dropped away. "Me." He turned away and opened his car door, climbing out.

I got out as well. My throat felt tight, and my chest hurt, but I'd lived through the death of both of my parents. I'd dealt with bullies in school. People in town snootily suggesting I wouldn't make a go of my ice cream shop.

I could handle this too.

He rounded the front of the car and stopped in front of me. "I'm sorry. I . . . I told myself I wasn't going to get involved with anyone."

"Never?" I traced my fingertip across my lips, wishing that he'd kissed me.

"For a while."

"How strong is your vow?"

"It's not quite a vow."

"A promise to yourself?"

"Not even that," he said.

"It's okay if you don't want to get involved with anyone." With me, that is. It hurt to think he didn't see right away that we might be good together.

"I'm not exactly saying that." He ran his fingers across the top of his head, messing up his hair.

I wouldn't push him. We barely knew each other. But minds could change . . .

He hefted his pad of paper and pen, fluttering them in the air. "Let's gather some evidence, and then we can talk."

Whenever a guy wanted to talk, it usually involved letting me down gently. So much for getting dirty.

"Sure." Faking a smile, I waved for him to go ahead of me up the paved walkway. "Grannie lives in the house. I'm in the apartment above the garage."

His gaze shot in that direction before landing on me again. I swore I read a hint of sadness there.

We went inside.

"Grannie?" I called out as I shut the back door. "I've brought Elrik from Monsters, PI. He'd like to ask you a few questions."

"I'm in the living room, dear," she said cheerfully. "Bring him in." Her voice lowered, and a hint of mischief came through. "From your description, I bet he's cute. Is he? I get so few visitors that it's nice when they're cute."

"What do you think?" I whispered. "Are you cute?"

He shot me a smile that made heat flare through me. "I believe I am cute. What do you think?"

I grumbled. "I think you're a guy with a promise he made not to get involved with anyone yet."

"Touché." He scratched the back of his neck, and his gaze dragged from mine to the floor as if he wasn't sure how I'd respond to his words. "I'm beginning to think I should relax my rule."

It was all I could do not to gush. "Truly?"

His gaze met mine again, his still quite serious. “Maybe.”

Maybe? Talk about mixed signals.

“This way.” I guided him out of the kitchen and down the short hall to the living room where Grannie Rose sat on the sofa, skeins of yarn around her and a partly finished mitten in her arthritic hands.

“He *is* cute.” Setting aside her knitting, she started to stand.

“Please, don’t get up.” He strode toward her, his hand extended. “I’m Elrik Nivalis. *I* think I’m cute.”

“See?” Grannie chuckled as she stared up at him. “I’m delighted to meet you in person, Elrik. You said you’re an ice lord?”

“Yes, Nivalis is a very old name, though it used to be common among the ice people.” He tapped his muscular forearm. “We all have light blue skin.”

“It’s quite attractive.” Her head tilted. “I’ve met various monsters since they decided to settle among humans, but I don’t believe I’ve ever met an ice lord. If you don’t mind me asking, what kind of monster is that?”

I was as interested in hearing what he had to say as my grandmother.

He waited for me to sit in the chair to Grannie’s right before settling beside my grandmother on the sofa.

His gaze held mine as he spoke. “Long ago, when the world was still young, it’s said there were gods who ruled over the natural elements. Among those deities were those whose hearts matched the cold harshness of winter itself.”

"The ice lords," Grannie breathed. She loved a good story as much as me.

"This isn't real, right?" He couldn't be a true god.

"This is my family's history as it's been told for many generations," he said without a hint of humor in his voice. "I'm real, so . . ."

"Let the poor man finish, Melly," Grannie said, though sweetly.

She might be stern with those in town, but she'd rarely scolded me. I'd done all I could to please her. After Mom died, the social worker told me I'd probably wind up in foster care. I decided that if anyone took me in, I'd not only behave, but I'd also be the perfect child. Then no one would reject me like my dad did.

"I understand having doubts about ice lord history," Elrik said. "I've certainly shared them with my family."

"Can you control the weather?" I asked.

"Not so far." His grin rose before falling. "My family used to live in frozen citadels nestled high within jagged mountain peaks in the coldest regions of Canada, where blizzards roar across the mountains and consume the plains."

"Amazing." Grannie's brown eyes sparkled with excitement.

"It's said ice lords controlled every flake of snow that fell on the planet, that we created each in its own unique shape. That we formed icicles sharper than swords. That even our homes were made of ice bluer than the Caribbean Sea."

"It must be true," Grannie said with a pert nod. "Someone has to do this for our world."

"My people have been slowly dying out, however." His gaze sought mine again before returning to my grandmother. "Long ago, we left our ice castles and moved into the valley. We married humans and slowly, the way of the ice lords died out."

"Aw." Grannie sighed. "Such a sacrifice to make to continue your species."

"Not completely. Some of us still maintain a few of the abilities of our forefathers."

"Do you?" I asked, intrigued. His hands had been cold on my cheeks. When I touched his arm, it felt equally chilly. Was all of him cooler than a human?

"I can't control the weather, but I can produce this." He held out his palm, frowning at it, and a small block of ice appeared.

Grannie gasped.

My eyes widened.

"It's mostly a parlor trick now," he said, sharing a smile between us. "Though I recently formed a wall of ice to stop someone from evading arrest. In times of great need, the skill sharpens. There's no other way to describe it."

"I can see where that would come in handy," Grannie said. "How do you make ice like that?"

"I pull the coldness from deep inside me." He glanced my way. "We have a lower body temperature. About ten degrees lower than a human's. But . . ."

Grannie leaned toward him; her eyes wide. "But?"

"It's said when an ice lord meets his fated mate, she thaws him."

"Truly?" I asked.

He nodded, his gaze gliding down my frame. I shouldn't shiver from such a simple gesture, but one look from him made everything inside me tingle.

"I hope a fated mate doesn't take away an ice lord's ability to make ice," Grannie said. "Because you need that skill in your line of work."

"That ability will never go away."

"Well, that's good then." She cocked her head to look up at him. She was so tiny compared to Elrik, she looked like a doll dressed in a housecoat. "Now you've left that cold climate and come all the way to Cape Cod."

"I needed a change," he said, his eyes on me again.

"Well, Mystic Harbor is lovely." Granny nodded pertly. "We're busy with tourists in the summer, but it's wonderful in the winter when it's just us locals." Her soft smile faded. "But you didn't come here to share your family history, though I greatly appreciate hearing about it. You also didn't come here to create an ice cube that's now melting in your hand."

He snorted and took it to the kitchen. It clinked when he tossed it into the sink. Returning, he sat beside Grannie again.

"You're here to make sure I don't end up in jail for hurting my friends," Grannie said sadly.

"You're not going to jail," I said. "I'm not allowing it to happen."

"I'm not either." Elrik grabbed the pad of paper and pen he'd dropped on the coffee table and placed them on his thighs. "Let's start in the beginning, shall we?"

6

ELRIK

I quizzed Grannie Rose for over an hour, only stopping for a bit while Melly served tea in a real pot with delicate cups and saucers. We ate cookies she'd made from scratch and talked about the weather while we shared our snack.

"I arrived at the church early to make sure I had time to make the punch," Grannie Rose said. "Melly drove me there and brought the supplies inside. I was the first to arrive; there wasn't anyone else there. In fact, we had to use the key hidden in a fake rock in the garden to get inside the function room attached to the side of the church."

"Melly said you asked her to leave you there alone," I said.

"Only because she filled in for me already." Rose beamed at Melly. "She's been so much help. I don't know what I would've done without her. But I'm getting stronger all the time, and I guess I'm stubborn enough that I wanted to do this on my own. It felt like it had been forever since I'd made my special punch."

"I planned to pick her up in about three hours," Melly said. "Grannie had a phone and would send a text when she was ready. Instead, I got a text telling me she was in jail and asking if I could please bail her out." She released a low shudder.

"I was just finishing up the punch when others started to arrive," Grannie said. "I had to go to the bathroom, and Sue was quite kind to help me." Her spine stiffened. "I handled things in the stall myself, of course, but it's good to have another person around when you're using a walker. Safety has to come first. "

"Sue helped you?" She nodded as I wrote it down. "How long were you in the bathroom?"

"Ten minutes or so. These things take time." Rose cleared her throat. "Like always, I made my special punch in the church's big bowl. Melly took it from the closet for me, washed it, and placed it on the buffet table before she left."

"Did you see anyone else around the building?" I asked Melly.

She shook her head. "There are no homes nearby, and it's wooded beyond the parking lot. I suppose someone could've been hiding in the trees or behind the church or function room. It didn't occur to me to look. There's next to no crime in Mystic Harbor. It's quite safe there."

"What happened next?" I asked Rose.

"Since my fall, I'm not as spry as I used to be," Grannie said. "It took me some time to get down the hall to the lady's room, do my thing, and return to the function room. By then, everyone had arrived, and let me tell you, it was a scene straight out of a nightmare. People were vomiting or staggering against the wall. My dear friend, Sue, collapsed on the wooden floor. I called 9-1-1 immediately, of course, and they sent an ambulance."

"You said you hold a potluck dinner. Had anyone started eating while you were gone?" Her punch might not have been the only tainted offering.

"No, we always wait until everyone's seated. We sip punch and chat a bit while the crockpots are heating things up, and then we fill our plates. They love my punch and can't resist getting into it right away. I never have to dump any out at the end of the evening." Her eyes filled with tears. "I poisoned my friends with my punch. Someone tampered with it while I was in the bathroom. I just know it."

"I think you're right," I said. "Who else came to the social that night?" Melly had given me the names, but she wasn't there. Others could've gone to the event, and I didn't want to miss anyone.

"The usual. Sue, my best friend all the way back to high school. She's quite the poker player." Grannie's spine tightened. "She occasionally beats me, though I will say that I've had a winning streak and haven't lost in over eight months."

Grannie was a poker shark; she should try her skills in Vegas.

"Alfred arrived with Sue," Grannie said, frowning. "They've been . . ." For whatever reason, her gaze fell to her lap where she fidgeted with a ball of yarn. "*Dating* for a year." Her brow furrowed. "Let me see. Carla was there. She's a widow. Her husband, Walter, was much older, and he left her a ton of money. He's been gone nearly ten years now."

I wrote that information down, though I wasn't sure how it could play into the investigation. "Was Ginny there?"

"My younger sister's stepdaughter?" Grannie said. "Only for a short time. She's Bob's caregiver, so she brings him to the event and then waits in the van." She tapped my leg. "My sister was much younger than me. Ginny's not a blood relation, though I did my best to treat her as if she was, at least until the divorce."

"How old is Ginny?" I asked.

"Her late twenties," Melly said.

"And Carla?"

"Thirty-seven." Grannie nodded pertly. "Walter was quite the catch, though as I said, he was much older than her. In his seventies to her twenty-three when they got married. When he passed, she was amply rewarded, though I'm not sure she'd agree."

"What does that mean?" I asked.

Grannie sipped her tea and placed her cup back on the coffee table. "I'm not sure anything will ever be enough for Carla. He left her a big estate on the ocean here in town, plus a home in Florida they traveled to in the winter. She prefers Cape Cod and is always worried a hurricane will go through and destroy the Florida place."

"Carla works with me at Creature Cones," Melly said. "She stopped by not long after I opened, and we somehow got talking about me hiring someone. I offered, and she seemed excited to be working with me. She said it would keep her busy, get her out of the house."

Grannie Rose grunted. "Walter was a horse fanatic. They went to all the races." She sniffed and wiggled her spine. "Carla got to wear all those stunning hats. You know the kind I mean. I was quite jealous of that." She patted the big gray bun neatly pinned to the top of her head. "I always wanted to wear one of those hats with fake fruit on it, but I didn't quite dare." Her hand landed on my knee, her grip tighter than I'd expect from such a tiny, frail-appearing woman. "Don't let life pass you by without doing the fun things you've always dreamed of. Wear that hat. Bungee jump off the cliff. Go ziplining. I wish I'd done it, but I believe I'm now too old for something like that." Her head tilted. "Maybe they have geriatric ziplines, and I could still fulfill that dream." Her cackle rang out. "I could wear a fruit hat while I did it."

"I bet you could." Perhaps I could look into that for her. First, I needed to clear her name. Second, I had to make things right with Melly, who I suspected might like me, and who I'd pretty much rejected in my fumbling attempt to tell her about the promise I'd made to myself to protect my heart after being hurt. Third . . . I was sure I could come up with something.

"Who else was there?" Grannie tapped the names off on her fingers. "Me. Alfred and Sue, Carla. Bob of course, as was Hazel. Bob's in his late sixties. He's a widower. His poor wife died, and he's had a tough time of it since. He said our church socials are the highlight of his life, that he looks forward to them all week long."

I wrote down the details. I could start looking into everything online tonight.

"Tell me about Hazel," I said.

Melly snorted, though I wasn't sure why. She offered me the last cookie on the plate, and I munched through it quickly. I loved peanut butter chocolate chip cookies.

"Hazel's seventy-two, and truly, she should retire." Grannie cackled. "Though I understand why she doesn't. Her work keeps her spry." Her hand flicked to her floral housecoat. "Look at me, only eighty and using a walker, though I'll point out that I'm still rehabilitating after my hip fracture and surgery. I plan to fling the walker aside as soon as I can and get around without it again."

I bet she would soon.

"What does Hazel do to keep herself spry?" I asked.

"She teaches pole dancing," Melly said, her eyes sparking. "She's amazing, actually. I shouldn't laugh. It's not the pole dancing or the fact that she's in her seventies while doing it, it's the fact that when she first came to Mystic Harbor, she wanted to offer *nude* pole dancing. The planning board's gasps were so loud, you could've heard them three towns over."

"I assume she wears clothing while she teaches," I said.

"Yes, she gave up that idea quickly," Grannie said. "She was quite the ballerina in her day until she was injured. I went to her first few classes when she opened her business here in town. It was fun, though I did worry about falling. I couldn't hold onto that pole no matter how hard I tried. There are mats underneath, but at my age, bones break much too easily."

"Grannie fell at the church function hall," Melly said. "She slipped on something left behind by the janitor. It was horrible."

"The local lawyer said I should sue," Grannie said. "But I'm not one to do something like that." She sipped the last of her tea and placed her cup and saucer on the coffee table again. "Maybe once I've tossed away my walker, I'll take another class and prove to that pole that I have what it takes to ride it and ride it hard."

Melly's eyes sparkled. "No pole dancing, Grannie. Please. You don't want to break your other hip."

"I suppose you're right," Rose said with a sigh. "I'll have to find something else I can do to get my body back into fighting shape."

"Fighting shape?"

"Grannie was one of the first women's kickboxers in the country," Melly said. "That was years ago, however, and she only competed in a few fights."

Grannie held up her fists. "Knocked 'em out on the regular. Don't let anyone ever tell you something different."

"You're amazing." Would she find it patronizing if I kissed her on the cheek? Probably. But before this case was through, I was going to do it.

Color rose into her wrinkled cheeks, and I could see where Melly got her beauty. "You're too kind."

"I only speak the truth."

She tapped my arm. "You're a sweet ice lord. I hope you find someone soon who will thaw your heart."

I thought that was my ex, but she hadn't warmed me. My gaze met Melly's. I was attracted to her, but that didn't mean anything. I'd compartmentalize my growing feelings like I did with everything else in my life and that would put perspective on the rushes of heat I felt whenever I looked her way.

After asking a few more questions, I announced it was time for me to go. I could see Grannie Rose was tired, and I hated to strain such a sweet old lady. "I'll stop by again tomorrow to ask more questions."

Melly and Grannie rose when I did. Inching forward with her walker, Grannie insisted on going with us to the door. I wanted to pick her up, plunk her back on the sofa, and do everything for her. This frail woman had not poisoned anyone, and for a moment, rage flushed through me. I wanted to snarl at whoever tried to frame her for this, then make sure they were locked up for a very long time.

"I appreciate you coming by and sharing my tea and cookies," she said in a chirpy voice. "And I look forward to your visit tomorrow." Her rheumy gaze went to Melly. "Perhaps we can talk him into coming to dinner soon."

"That's up to Elrik," Melly said.

I kept remembering her saying she enjoyed getting dirty, and that made me want to tease her about what she might serve.

I also wanted to kiss her.

Was I letting my simple promise to myself hold me back?

"I'd love to come for dinner," I said. "I don't get a home-cooked meal very often."

"See?" Grannie nodded my way, her gray bun at the peak of her head bobbing along with the action. "We can cook him something special. Do you have any food allergies? Is there anything you dislike?"

"I love everything, and no, no allergies," I said.

"I'm going to drive Elrik back to the office, and I'll come right home after that," Melly said.

"Don't rush on my behalf," Grannie Rose said. "I want to complete a few more rows on that mitten."

Odd weather to be knitting mittens.

"I make them all year long," she said as if she'd read my mind. "I donate them to the church for their annual fundraiser. My mittens are in hot demand. People literally fight over them." She waved to a plaque hanging on the wall. "I've been honored with the church's Good Citizen Award four years running for my mitten donations." Her smile lifted. "Boy does that make Sue mad. She used to win with her prized wood carving ornaments, but once I started producing mittens, it was over." She laughed, but her smile faded. "I hope she's released from the hospital soon. I hate to think she could be in pain."

"I called the hospital," Melly said. "They told me she's going home tomorrow."

Grannie clapped. "Wonderful. I'm so relieved to hear that." Pausing in the kitchen, she frowned. "You know what just occurred to me? I need to see if I can find some patterns online for monster-sized mittens. That'll up my mitten game and ensure I win the award again this year." Her gaze traveled to my hands. "Could I take some measurements? As a lord of the ice, you're a chilly man, and I'm sure you like being cold, but I'd love to make you some mittens that match your eyes."

"I'd love to wear your mittens," I said, grinning along with Melly. "I'll be happy to let you take whatever measurements you need. Just let me know when."

"How about when you come to dinner?" She tugged out a kitchen chair and sat. "I could take measurements then."

"Would the day after tomorrow work for you?" Melly asked. "I'll make something special."

"That sounds great."

We left, Melly and I walking out to her car, where we got inside.

"Your grandmother is amazing," I said as she drove back through town. "She's also cute."

"She is." Melly shot me a smile. She pulled into the lot across from Monsters, PI, and parked. After unbuckling, she turned to face me. "Thank you for being patient with her. I hope you learned a few things that could lead to clues."

I tapped the pad of paper I'd placed on my lap. "I have suspects already. Are you free tomorrow to go with me to question some of them?"

She frowned. "I'm working, of course. New business and all that. But I imagine Carla could cover for a few hours in the morning. We're busier after lunch."

"Carla, the widow who married the much older man and then inherited all his wealth?"

"Yup, that's the one. Would you believe she was my babysitter when I was young? Grannie had her come stay with me after school and before Grannie got home from work until I turned fourteen. Then I convinced Grannie I was safe enough at home alone with the doors locked.

Carla and I used to watch a lot of TV." Her lips squished together before she spoke. "She was a college student back then. I'm twenty-eight, and she's nine years older than me."

"And now she works with you at Creature Cones." Which was a few doors down from Monsters, PI. I'd noted it once or twice but hadn't stopped in for ice cream yet. Actually, I also realized Hazel's studio, Boogey Beasts, was right next to Creature Cones. I hadn't realized Boogey Beasts taught pole dancing. I'd seen kids in sparkling costumes coming and going and assumed the owner only taught dance.

"Carla doesn't need to work," Melly said. "A month ago, she stopped by for ice cream, and we reconnected. She said she was bored. I said I needed help, and she offered. I hired her on the spot. She works from ten until four, and she's off Monday and Tuesday."

"I'll interview her first, then. Is it okay if I come in early enough tomorrow to ask her a few questions before she has to cover for you?"

"I think that'll work well." She placed her hand on my arm. My skin twitched and suddenly warmed from her palm, but it was hot in the car sitting in the sun. "Thank you. I don't know what I'd do without you."

"Grannie Rose is not going to jail." I gave her a sharp nod. "I promise."

7

MELLY

The next morning, I was finishing setting up the cute, white-painted cast iron tables and chairs in front of Creature Cones when I spied Elrik striding across the street from the parking lot. Sunlight hit his dark hair just right, making it rival the wings of a raven soaring across a moonlit sky.

"Hottie alert," Carla breathed from beside me.

I'd explained that Elrik was coming by today.

Carla watched Elrik approach with a slight curl of her lips. "*This* is the investigator helping you with Grannie's case? If so, I take it back. I'm not irritated that he wants to question me any longer. In fact, maybe he and I could go get coffee or take a drive along the coast. While he's questioning me, that is. I promise." She flashed me a mischievous smile. "I won't be gone *too* long."

"He's not interested in a relationship," I barked before lowering my voice. "That's the impression I get, that is." There was no way I was going to share what he told me about his ex.

"Maybe he can be persuaded to change his mind." As he strode down the sidewalk, she sauntered toward him, her hips swaying and her long red hair swaying across her back. When he'd nearly reached her, she held out her hand. "I'm Carla Whitten." Her voice came out smooth, yet breathy in a way only Carla could pull off. I envied the ability and assumed this was the voice that had roped in Walter. "I understand you'd like to . . . talk with me?"

"Yes, I would." As his fingers touched hers, his gaze sought mine, and I swore it softened when he found me. Or the sunlight hit them just right, and I was mistaken. His hand dropped to his side. "Why don't we go inside? This won't take long." He eased around her.

"I'm happy to help in any way I can." She stared at his backside before grinning at me and sashaying after him.

He paused by me. "Good morning, Melly. Nice to see you."

There was nothing better than the drawl of a hot ice lord.

"Morning," I croaked. My face overheated. This wasn't a competition, but couldn't I just once sound sultry when I wanted to instead of coming across like a frog lounging on the muddy bank of the river?

He gave me a full smile that made everything inside me slide away like an avalanche tumbling down a hillside. When I nearly toppled against the brick front of Creature Cones, his hand snapped out to hold me steady. "Careful there. Did you trip?"

Only my heart. "I think so."

Carla watched us from inside, her lips thinning. "I thought you had questions for me, *Investigator*."

"Oh, I do," he said. "Have a seat. I'll be with you shortly."

With a huff, she banged the front door closed and moved across the room.

A group of eight people, a mix of humans and monsters and of various ages, smiled as they passed us, going inside for ice cream. Carla would handle them until I could join her. I wanted to spend a few seconds with Elrik.

"Did everything go alright last night?" he asked.

I'd slept horribly. I kept dreaming of him, something I suspected wouldn't go over well if I mentioned it. "Fine," I said instead. "Grannie's doing okay. Now that you're on the case, she feels much better about the future." And that was the most important thing, not my crush on Investigator Ice Lord.

"I tossed and turned all night," he said, releasing my arm. He frowned at his hand, flexing his fingers and turning his hand this way and that.

"Is your hand alright?" I didn't see a cut there or any reason for concern.

"Yes." He tucked it into his jeans pocket and flashed me a smile. "Let me talk with Carla and then we can leave."

At my nod, he went inside. I followed, taking over from Carla, who sauntered over to sit at a table across from him.

While I helped the rest of the customers, I kept my ears cocked in their direction, trying to listen in on their conversation. My insides kept twisting into a knot and releasing. I wanted to rip out all of Carla's pretty sunset hair. Claw her face.

Jealousy didn't taste any better than dirt ice cream.

I served a basilisk a double scoop waffle cone and rang up his order. Smiling, I took care of the next customer, an older woman with bright pink hair.

Elrik asked Carla some basic questions about the church social. She'd arrived not long after Sue and Alfred, though she only knew they were there because their jackets had been hung on the peg by the door. She'd placed her crockpot full of barbecued mini weenies on the table near Grannie's punch. And no, she hadn't seen anyone doing anything suspicious with the drink.

"Everyone else arrived after me," she said, laying her hand on the table near his. Her four-karat diamond ring flashed in the sunlight streaming in from the big window beside them, the sparkle nearly blinding me.

I ran the last customer up and held my smile until they'd left. The door had barely closed before a yeti family of four came in and placed their order. Like usual, this place was hopping. With the sun shining and my location on Main Street, it wasn't uncommon to have a line out the door and partway down the street. This was why I'd opened Creature Cones in this building, though Grannie gave me a great deal on the rent. Long ago, she'd run an accounting office here, but she let me renovate the space and open my own business.

Fortunately, I was doing great. I could not only make the decent rent I insisted on paying, but I was also able to put some of the profit aside for business savings. Cape Cod was busy in the summer, and almost everyone loved ice cream. I even offered ten different dairy- and gluten-free varieties for those who were intolerant.

Elrik finished with Carla, and it didn't sound like he'd obtained much information from her. While he remained seated, she rose and came over to stand with me as the next customers, a human couple in their sixties, strode toward the counter.

"Are you sure you're okay with me leaving you here alone?" I asked Carla. "It's busy."

"Nothing odd about that, right?" She smiled at the woman. "What can I get you, hun?"

The woman studied the offerings. "How about a double cone with a scoop of coconut and a scoop of chocolate?"

We served thirty-two different flavors, and I purchased our stock from a small local supplier who also crafted a few exclusive blends solely for me. Everyone loved what we served at Creature Cones; there had even been a write-up about us in the Boston Globe. Business was even steady during the off-season.

"Coming right up." Carla opened the sliding glass door and grabbed a scoop, nodding my way. "Go. I've got this covered." She crooked her finger, and I bent close for her to whisper. "That guy only has eyes for you. I envy you, hun. He's gorgeous, nice, and rich from what I saw."

"What makes you think he has money?"

She placed a generous ball of coconut on the cone and aimed for the chocolate. "I'd recognize designer clothing and shoes anywhere."

"Maybe he's a savvy thrift store shopper. People dump

stuff like that there all the time." Especially on Cape Cod where many of the wealthy retired.

"Did he thrift a home on the ocean?"

"He has a place on the water?"

"He casually mentioned it—when I asked." She squished a scoop of chocolate on top of the coconut and handed the cone to the woman, smiling toward the man who was still studying the chalkboard listing all the flavors we offered. "I know the place. It's gorgeous," she said softly to me. "A real estate friend told me the new owner paid cash for it."

Stuff like that didn't matter to me. I cared more for the person behind the money or the lack thereof.

"He's a nice guy," was all I said.

Her smile grew. "I trained you well."

"I thought you married Walter because you loved him."

Tears filled her eyes, and I swore they weren't fake. "I did. The money was just a bonus." She pinched her eyes shut before opening them again. "I still miss him. I hear him calling my name, but when I turn, he's not there." Her long sigh rang out. "He's never there. I was cheated. I deserved more than four years with the love of my life."

"You did."

After wiping her eyes, she flapped her hands my way. "Go do some investigation with Elrik. You take your time, hun. Have coffee if you want, since he turned me down. I bet he'll say yes to you." She leaned into my side. "You deserve to find a good guy, and I suspect that's him."

"I told you he's not interested in a relationship with anyone."

"Then he shouldn't look at you like he'd like to kiss you."

Before I could reply to that, she nudged me around the counter and spoke to Elrik. "Have her back before dark or I'm coming after you." She pointed her finger playfully at him before lifting it and blowing off the pretend smoke from her finger weapon. "I mean it, you hear?"

I cringed.

Elrik laughed and got up, opening the door for me to step outside while she took a customer's ice cream order.

We crossed the road.

"Ride with me," he said, going around to open the passenger door of his enormous truck parked next to my car. "There's no need to take two vehicles."

"Okay." Before I could figure out how I'd crook my leg up enough to place my foot on the running board, Elrik spanned my waist with his big hands and lifted me into the seat. He stepped onto the running board and buckled me in, frowning at me after the buckle clicked.

"Thank you." My skin still burned where he'd touched me, and the fabric of my sundress had been between us. Flustered, I smoothed the skirt across my thighs.

"No problem." His gaze remained on my mouth long enough I began to wonder if my lipstick was smeared or if . . . Nah, he didn't want to kiss me. He'd made a promise to himself, and while he might be reconsidering it, the desire to do so had to come from him. I was going to do all I could to keep from tempting him into doing something he might not be ready for yet.

"Are we going to leave?" I finally asked.

He shook his head and jumped to the ground. "Sorry."

"No problem."

He shut the door, and my hungry eyes tracked him as he moved around the hood and climbed into the driver's seat. After staring forward for a moment, he buckled and started the vehicle with a roar.

"Who do you plan to interview first?" I asked.

"I called the church and got permission to go inside the function room adjacent to the church. They told me where they hid the key. I want to look around before we head to the hospital. Sue's going home today, but when I called, she said she and Alfred expected they'd be there until late morning. They want to check her lab work one more time before releasing her."

"Do you think we'll find anything in the function room that Detective Carter hasn't already seen?"

He shrugged as he turned the vehicle onto the road with the church at the end. "We're going to find out."

We parked in the empty lot and went inside, turning on the lights.

"Look around," he said. "Call out if you see anything interesting."

I nodded. "They confiscated the church's punch bowl. I think Grannie was as pissed about that as the fact that they arrested her. Since she's used it so often, she considers it hers."

"When this is over, we'll get it back." He rounded the table where the food and drinks were always set up and bent over to look in the trash bucket behind.

I hoped this would be over with soon, that we'd discover who put the Xylitol in the punch and why they'd tried to frame my grandmother for the crime.

"Nothing in the trash." He waved to the door on the back wall. "What's through there?"

"A kitchen. If someone comes early, like they often do around the holidays when they need to decorate, they can prepare their food there rather than bring it ready to serve."

"Six is a small group for something like that." He strode toward the door, and I followed. I'd found nothing suspicious so far, but the place would've been cleaned by the janitor—who we could also question.

"The church congregation is much larger, but only a small group gets together weekly for the social club. This group of six have been meeting here every single Saturday night for years."

"Amazing." He opened the door to the kitchen and waved for me to enter ahead of him.

I stepped inside, taking in the water-stained wooden table, metal chairs, and a green vinyl counter that looked like it had been there since the 1970s. "Do you play poker?"

"I don't."

I grinned up at him. "Maybe once this is over, we could come to a social and give it a try. I've only joined them a few times. When she wins, which is most of the time, Grannie crows and hops around—as much as she can with her walker, now—and Sue snarls. Sue hates losing. She swears Grannie cheats, though in a good way.

They're besties, so she really isn't pissed off at my grandmother."

"It sounds like a lot of fun. Maybe I *will* join the group."

"You'd be more than welcome."

He stroked my hair off my face. "I believe I want to kiss you."

My breath caught. Maybe he *was* interested in a relationship. "That's a switch."

"I've been thinking."

"Sometimes, thinking's a good thing. Other times, not so much."

"Would you like me to kiss you?"

"Very much. I assume you're speaking of only one kiss?"

His eyes smoldered. "I think I'd like to do a lot more than kiss you, Melly."

I wanted to tug up his shirt, lean against his chest, and nuzzle my face in his skin. I resisted and put distance between us, turning toward the kitchen cabinets.

"No kiss?" he asked.

"You're the one who promised himself he wasn't going to start anything new."

"So much for that," I swore he muttered.

"What?" I asked over my shoulder.

His gaze was focused on my ass. "Nothing. Absolutely nothing."

8

ELRIK

How had I ever thought I could tell myself I wouldn't get involved with someone new?

That was before I met Melly. I never thought I'd meet anyone who would appeal to me as much as my ex. Now I could barely remember what Brittney looked like. All I could see was Melly's inky hair that gleamed almost blue in the lights, her hazel eyes that were brown when she gazed at her grandmother with love and held a hint of green when they turned toward me. What did the green mean, and should I be hoping they'd flash brown one of these days when she looked my way?

"What would you think of a guy who broke a promise he'd made to himself?" I asked as I opened the fridge and looked inside. Completely empty. Closing it, I opened the cupboards, finding nothing except a box of baking soda, half-full salt and pepper shakers, plus packages of paper plates, cups, and plasticware.

"I assume you're speaking of your promise to avoid relationships for the time being."

"Yes, that."

"It's up to you. When you promised yourself, I'm sure you had a solid reason. You didn't want to set yourself up to be hurt again, and I get it. None of us want something like that. But as for breaking your promise . . ." Turning, she leaned back against the counter. "Only you can decide when it's time to try again."

"I think I'm ready."

"Think?" With a sigh, she spun and stared out the window above the sink. "When you're sure one way or the other, you'll act. You won't stand around thinking about it."

She was right. Was I ready? The pain I'd felt when my brother and Brittney announced to everyone they were not only together but that they were getting married had faded. I could barely remember the dismay and sadness that had wracked through me back then.

I thought I loved her, but the feelings I'd had for her couldn't compare to the warmth and excitement I felt whenever I was with Melly.

Was I ready? Rebound relationships never worked. I'd read that somewhere.

This doesn't have to be a rebound; it can be for forever, my heart insisted.

Maybe it was right.

I went over to look out the window myself, taking in the back lot with no vehicles and the scraggly woods beyond.

"When I was a kid, Grannie brought me here every Sunday afternoon for a church youth group. We spent more time running through the woods and telling each other spooky stories than studying the bible."

"Good memories, though."

She smiled up at me. "The best."

I stepped to the cupboards to the right of the sink and opened them, finding them empty.

Melly opened the doors beneath the sink and dropped to her knees, poking her head into the dark space.

Her ass was cute. Ripe and lush. I wanted to put my hands on it, feel it naked. She wore a sundress today, a sleeveless one that showed off her arms. It was cut low enough in the front to hint at the swell of her breasts, and my stupid cock had started to stir when I focused on that area as I walked up to her in front of Creature Cones. The dress had big sunflowers all over it, and I loved how cheery it was, how carefree and pretty—just like this woman.

I especially adored how the hem rode up on her thighs while she wiggled around beneath the sink.

"Let me do that," I said, stooping down beside her.

She jerked her head back, hitting it on the pipes, and yelped.

I spanned my fingers around her waist, loving how lush she was even here, and tugged her carefully out of the space. Sitting with my back to the cupboards and my legs stretched out in front of me, I placed her on my lap, facing me. This meant she had to straddle my thighs.

My cock liked that almost as much as it did the swell of her breasts. Which were right in front of me.

After watching her swallow go down hard, I dragged my attention to her face.

"Are you alright?" I rubbed the back of her head, finding no bump. "You're not dizzy, are you?"

"What if I was?" she said, her lips twitching upward before smoothing. "Would you perform CPR? That wouldn't qualify as kissing. I doubt anyone would say it broke the promise you made to yourself."

"About that."

"I'm sure it made sense at the time."

When she didn't meet my eye, I gently lifted her chin and stared into her eyes. Green with hints of brown. "It did make sense."

"You were hurt. Cheating with your brother is just about the biggest betrayal out there."

"It is."

"She should've ended things with you before starting something with him. And him! There should be a brother code or something that forbids someone from stealing a sibling's girlfriend."

"He apologized."

"After the fact."

"They tried to tell me. I was away on a rescue mission. It happened while I was gone."

"Things like that don't just happen. They take intent."

"You're right."

"I'm sorry. I'm sure you loved her a lot."

I swore her eyes searched mine. What did she hope to find there?

"We were a couple for six months before she met my brother. I should've seen it developing between them. All the signs were there. They were both so awkward together when she came for Christmas dinner. They kept looking at each other, then jerking their gazes away. We all grew up together, though he's older than us. I don't think he noticed she was around until the holiday. Then, he saw her."

"Did his skin heat for her?"

I shrugged. "If it did, he hasn't shared that with me. They told me when I got back from my mission."

"She stayed there with him while you were gone?"

"I live only a few towns away from my brother's place, but yeah."

"Were you . . ." She pinched her eyes shut, and when she opened them, they searched mine even harder. "Did you two . . ." Her growl ripped out. "Sorry. I shouldn't ask that. It's none of my business."

"We didn't, actually."

Her head tilted. "Why not if you were together for six months?"

"I'm not sure why we didn't. I was away a lot with my job. She was busy too. She's a lawyer and in court a lot."

"I'm sorry it didn't work out for you two."

"I'm not." For the first time in months, I could say that and truly mean it.

"Why not?"

I was taking a chance here. We'd only met a short time ago. But she had the right to know what I'd confirmed this morning.

I met her gaze. "Because my skin has heated for you."

9

MELLY

I couldn't breathe. I could barely think. All I could do was press my fingertips into his forearms. Stroke them with my palms and press deeply as if I could sink beneath his skin and feel the warmth he spoke of.

I was perched on his lap with my thighs spread around his hips, my knees pressing against the counter behind him. My skirt had hitched up high enough he could probably see my undies if he squinted in that direction.

"Heat. You said that . . ." If I spoke the words aloud, would that break them?

"That when an ice lord meets his fated mate, his cold heart warms. Everything inside him heats up and stays that way."

"Fated mate?" I flashed my gaze up to meet his, and I found fire there.

For me.

"About that promise." I was borrowing his words, but

I couldn't help it. "How badly would you feel if you broke it?"

"My word means a lot to me but . . ."

But was the best word in the world.

"But what?" I croaked. Damn frogs were at it again, sunning themselves by the river.

"I'm desperate to kiss you."

"Are you asking or making a statement?" I couldn't hold his gaze. What if I saw glaciers in his eyes now instead of the heat I swore I'd seen before?

"A question. It's always polite to ask," he growled.

Maybe he really did want to kiss me.

"We can, um . . ." There were times when spontaneity worked wonders.

I rose onto my knees, latched onto his shoulders, and planted my mouth on his. This way, he wasn't breaking the word he'd given himself. I was doing it for him instead. Semantics, but still.

A twist, and he lay on the rug spanning the wooden floor in front of the sink with me lying on top of him. His tongue stroked my lips and made demands I was very eager to give in to.

His warm hands stroked up and down my back, and when he cupped my ass and squeezed, a growl ripped up his throat.

His mouth was pure bliss. Kissing him filled a part of me inside I hadn't realized was empty.

I tugged up his shirt, wiggling myself around on his body to get it up enough I could touch his skin. He was hot. A regular inferno. And I was dry wood and paper, poised to ignite.

I lifted my head, locking my gaze on his, finding flames there, as if he'd captured white-hot lightning and trapped it within his soul.

"You taste amazing," he said.

"We um, probably shouldn't be doing this here. We're pretty much inside a church. Lying on the kitchen floor in front of a sink."

"Not the place I'd ever want to claim my fated mate."

Claim? I had a feeling that involved more than kisses.

Oh, my. I fanned my face because I was the one feeling hot now. I scrambled off him and stood while he sat, staring up at me.

"I didn't make you uncomfortable, did I?" he asked.

"You were the one lying on the ratty rug in front of the sink."

"I'd happily lie on mud if you were on top of me."

He rose to his feet and took my hands.

"You didn't make me uncomfortable," I said. "I worried I was doing that to you."

"Never happening." He gave me a smile that made my knees tremble. "I'm declaring myself for you, Melly. Are you ready to be courted by an ice lord?"

Once again, I could barely think, so I nodded.

"Good girl," he said.

I'd never thought I was one who enjoyed praise kink, but if I could be Elrik's good girl, I was all over it.

"What does being courted by an ice lord entail?" And where was he going with this? Claiming meant dating, right? Kisses. Maybe some touching, but . . .

There was no such thing as fated mates.

Except his skin was icy when I first met him, and now he was hotter than an oven.

"I'm going to pursue you until you tell me you want everything," he said.

I lifted my eyebrows. "Everything?"

"My heart. My future. My children if the fates grant them to us. My ring on your finger. My cock buried deep inside your body. My kisses. My home and hearth and the heat that's blazing inside me only for you."

"That's a lot to take in all at once." But my skin felt as hot as his now. My body had gone melty. And I suspected when his cock was buried deep inside my body, I was going to cry out his name.

"That's why we're going to finish up here, go talk to Sue and Alfred, and then I'm going to take you back to Creature Cones."

"There's no courting in that statement." Let alone cock.

"I'm working on it." He gave me a crooked smile. "We'll have dinner with your grandmother tomorrow night, and then . . ."

I tilted my head. "Then . . .?"

"What do you think of a date involving ice?"

10

ELRIK

"Do you mean something like swans slowly melting on a table at a fancy buffet?" she asked. "Or using molds to make ice cubes that look like dice?"

"Neither."

"Tell me."

I shot her a smile. "Do you like ice?"

She shook her head. "I guess so?"

"I'm an ice lord. Surely you can come up with a better answer than I guess so."

"Insulted you, did I?" she said with a low laugh.

"I'm going to surprise you, sweetheart. Wait and see."

"Then I can't wait until you present your surprise."

From the moment I met Melly, some part of me had known she would come to mean the world to me. We hadn't touched at the wedding, and it wasn't until she was sitting in my office that I felt something unexpected awaken inside me.

But her kiss . . . that had solidified everything in my mind and in my soul.

She was my fated mate, the one person I never expected to find. Now I was determined to court her and claim her.

We finished looking around inside of the function hall, but we didn't find anything suspicious.

Locking up, we walked to my truck, and I lifted her inside again, buckling her. This time, I paused to kiss her, and it wasn't long before she was moaning and clinging to my shoulders. I could kiss this woman all day and night and still end up needing to kiss her again.

Finally, I lifted my head.

She gave me a blissful smile. "You're good at that."

"I'm good at a lot of things."

Her eyes sparkled, and fuck, they were brown now. Was that a good sign? "I'm sure you are. Or you think you are," she added pertly. "Every guy says that. Very few deliver."

"There's time yet." I could tell myself I wasn't going to open my heart to anyone, that I would hold myself back and give myself time to heal. But all I wanted was Melly. By my side. In my bed. Smiling up at me with everything she felt for me blazing in her brown eyes. I embraced the feeling like a man standing on the shore with his arms wide while a big frothy wave crashed over him.

"I want to kiss you forever," she said. "But we have to interview Sue and Alfred before they leave the hospital, then get me back to Creature Cones so I can help Clara. She's going to start wondering what happened to me."

I'd happened to her, and I was quite proud of the fact.

After I'd buckled, I pressed down on the brake pedal and pushed the button on the dashboard to start the truck.

Nothing happened.

"Odd." I pushed it again. Still nothing.

"What's going on?" Melly asked, a thread of concern coming through in her voice. "You didn't run out of gas, did you?"

"Full tank. The truck's new. It only has a few thousand miles on it." I unbuckled and left the truck, walking around the vehicle to the hood. Melly slid from her seat and joined me.

An odd, sweet smell drifted through the air.

I glanced her way. "Someone cut my radiator hoses and disconnected the battery." I nudged my chin toward an index card lying on the engine. "They also left a calling card."

Melly stood on her tiptoes to read the black letters scrolling across the white card, but I could see them quite well from here.

Stop investigating.

Or else.

I LEFT everything alone and called Detective Carter, who said he'd be here shortly. I also called Cryptid Car Care and they said they'd send someone out with parts to do a quick repair here in the lot. They'd also make sure nothing else had been sabotaged.

We sat in the truck. Melly fretted. I studied the building, looking for cameras.

"We're not giving up," Melly said in a shrill voice. "Whoever framed Grannie Rose is not getting away with this."

"I won't stop until they're the ones worried about going to jail."

"Thank you." Her lower lip trembled.

I scooted across the bench seat and lifted her onto my lap, wrapping my arms around her. "We're going to clear her name."

"We've barely started looking for clues and this happens. What motive do they have for poisoning six people? And why try to blame Grannie?"

"Your grandmother could be collateral damage. They may have been trying to hurt one of the others, and her punch was convenient. No one would suspect a thing if a drink made with sherbet was extra sweet. They'd think she just messed up the recipe, something that wouldn't be unusual for someone her age."

"Never Grannie. She doesn't have even one sign of dementia or Alzheimer's. Not yet anyway. Her mother was sharp until she died at the age of ninety-two."

"Your grandmother is fortunate."

"I feel like time is ticking away and we're not making progress," she said. "I'm not criticizing you. I know you did some investigating last night, and you'll fill me in on what you found. But I'm worried. What if we can't find any evidence pointing to someone other than my grandmother?"

"I'm not going to let that happen."

She looked up at me. "I appreciate that. I'm grateful you're helping me figure this out. But some people are very good at hiding their tracks."

"There will be clues. We'll put them together."

Detective Carter pulled in at the same time as the wrecker. After giving the yeti mechanic the go-ahead, she started replacing the hoses and looking at the engine to make sure nothing else had been sabotaged. She also took care of the battery.

Detective Carter removed and bagged the note. "I don't know if I'll discover any clues from paper."

The note was written in block letters with what looked like a permanent marker.

"There are no cameras on the building or in the lot," I said.

"Good observation." Detective Carter squinted around the empty parking lot. "And they hide a key in a fake rock. I don't think there's anyone in town who doesn't know where it is."

I'd thought the same thing. They should install a door with a code or restrict access. Have someone let them in. There were plenty of things that would make the place safer.

Detective Carter grunted. "I've told all the businesses in town that they need to come up to speed on security, but most ignore me."

"The church isn't wealthy," Melly said. "They probably can't afford to add cameras."

"And look what happens." He held up the clear bag. "I'll ask around to see if anyone passed the lot and saw someone near your truck, but with the long driveway, the odds are slim."

I'd already noted this.

The detective frowned at the plastic bag a moment more before his gaze slid to Melly. "I told you I'm looking into the poisoning."

"You did." Wisely, she didn't say anything else.

His attention fell on me. "You're the new guy at Monsters, PI. The ice lord."

I nodded. "Elrik Nivalis."

"What exactly *is* an ice lord?"

Melly stiffened and huffed.

"I didn't mean anything by it." Detective Carter had the grace to wince. "I've just never heard of ice lords before."

"There aren't many of us left. Most live in northern Canada. But you know what I can do."

"That wall of ice you created to stop the thief from getting away with stealing Angie's kegs of beer *was* impressive."

"Thanks."

Angie had come to Monsters, PI after her specialty kegs of beer were stolen right before an important brew-off contest. My coworker, Tuvid, a gargoyle, had taken the case and solved it. Now he and Angie were married. Their relationship had progressed fast, too fast some might say. Not me. Many monsters knew right away when someone was the one, and Tuvid and Angie were fated mates. Why waste time when you know from the start that the other person is the one you'll love forever?

I caressed Melly with my eyes, taking in the pink

color in her pretty cheeks, the way the skirt of her sundress flirted with her thighs, and the brown color in her eyes when she looked at me.

She was mine. We were fated. I suspected we also wouldn't waste any time before making sure the world knew we were meant to be together.

"Did Melly hire you?" Detective Carter asked, drawing my attention back to him.

"She sure did."

The detective's lips thinned. "What have you discovered? While I don't like the idea of anyone blundering around in my case and messing things up, I assume you'll share everything you learn with me."

"Of course." Eventually.

"I've barely started." He scowled at Melly. "There was no need to hire a private firm. I told you I'd look into everything."

"And I told you my grandmother was not going to jail." The steel in Melly's voice would've frozen my blood if such a thing was possible.

Detective Carter didn't even flinch. "Yes, you did." He studied us both before grunting. "I'll see you two around." We watched as he sauntered over to his vehicle and got inside, driving it slowly out of the lot and toward town.

"Did you discover anything online?" Melly asked me.

I nudged my head to the vehicle, and we got inside, shutting the doors.

The mechanic finished and closed the hood, coming around to my window that I put down.

Her pale green eyes scanned us both. "All set." She

ran my card on a small machine and gave me a salute before getting into her tow truck and leaving.

"I'll tell you what I found later. We need to question Sue and Alfred before she's discharged."

"Alright."

I started my truck and drove to the hospital, parking in the lot. We went inside, and the front desk directed us to Sue's room.

We were about to push on Sue's cracked-open door until a nurse stopped beside us and tapped my arm. "Could you give her a second? She's in the bathroom. She should be right out."

"Sure."

We leaned against the wall, watching as a physical therapist helped an orc move down the hall. He used a walker, and from the way he hitched his gait, I suspected he'd done something to his left leg. Maybe he'd had surgery. At the other end of the hall, an elf pulled a covered food tray from a big silver cart and took it into one of the rooms. Late lunch or an early dinner?

"I never should've married you," a woman said inside Sue's room.

Melly's wide gaze met mine, and she whispered. "That's Sue. She's not married."

"You're the one who insisted on the Elvis wedding," a male said.

"That's Alfred." Melly's eyes grew even wider. "They're married?"

Did this somehow tie into what happened? An assumption like that would be a stretch, but I wasn't leaving any possible clue unexplored.

"Grannie never told me they'd gotten married," Melly added softly. "She and Sue are best friends. Maybe Grannie *doesn't* know."

"I hate Elvis, but I love you," Sue said. "If I hadn't drank all that free champagne at the casino, I might not have taken a peek inside the chapel."

"It was fun having the Elvis impersonator marry us," Alfred said.

"Do you think it's legal?" Melly whispered.

I shrugged. "I'll see if I can find the license online later."

She nodded, and we leaned toward the door. We should knock. Go inside now that Sue was out of the bathroom. But I suspected the conversation would end abruptly, and we might need to hear what they said.

"I love you," Alfred said in a pleading voice. "I have almost since we met at the pharmacy all those years ago."

"He's a retired pharmacist," Melly said.

"I love you too," Sue said with a sigh. "But you cheated on me!"

Melly's eyes grew even wider.

"I apologized," Alfred said. "It was just a kiss."

"A kiss is still cheating," Sue huffed. "And with Carla, of all people."

Carla?

Melly's wide-eyed gaze met mine.

"You said you forgave me," Alfred said.

Sue sighed. "I did. You're right."

"I only want you, sweetheart," Alfred said. "Not Carla."

"That gold digger," Sue snarled.

"She's not," he said. "She's just lonely."

"Then she needs to find some friends because she can't have you." Sue sighed. "I'm sorry we haven't spent a lot of time together lately. Things have been tough. There's so much to take care of all the time."

"That's why I've offered to help you," Alfred said. "Over and over again."

I'd done some research online last night. Sue was a retired kindergarten teacher.

"I know you have, and I appreciate it," she said.

"First things, first. I brought the paperwork with me. The pen's lying next to it."

"Where do I sign?"

"At the bottom," he said.

"*This* should show you I forgive you more than anything else," she said. "I kept adding to it like that man suggested, and for such a long time. It's certainly grown. I still think I should donate at least part of it to the library."

"I promise I'll make a donation in your name. The library's wonderful for this community, but we need to look out for each other first."

"You're right." I heard a scratching sound like a pen on paper. "Could you help me get onto the bed? I'll lay down until the nurse says it's time for me to leave."

"Of course, sweetheart," he said. "You won't regret this."

Footsteps approached our way.

We scooted to the side and leaned against the wall.

I heard a rustle of fabric as he helped her.

The nurse scooted over to us. "She must be done by now. Give us a sec, and I'll call out. You can come in after that. She's leaving soon, though. I've already gone through her discharge instructions. Her boyfriend is here to take her home." She cracked the door and slipped inside.

Boyfriend? Why hadn't the nurse named Alfred as Sue's husband? And why didn't the whole town know they were married?

When Melly's glance met mine, I could tell the same thoughts were crossing her mind.

The nurse opened the door again and gestured to us. "Come on in. I'm going to pack her things, and I'll get a wheelchair and someone to take her to the front door soon."

"We don't need much time," I said, urging Melly inside the room ahead of me.

"Hello," Sue said, smiling Melly's way. She'd dressed in dark pants and a loose white shirt and lay on top of the blankets. Her long gray hair had been secured in a ponytail at her nape, and her pale blue eyes sparkled. "It's sweet of you to stop by." Her gaze slid to me, and her smile remained true. "You must be Elrik. It's nice to meet you."

A raised table spanned the opposite side of the bed, holding a plastic water pitcher, a glass half-full of water, and a pile of papers resting on top of a manilla envelope.

"Thanks for letting us stop by to ask you a few questions," I said as I eased around the foot of the bed, determined to get close enough to see what the papers might reveal, if anything.

Sue's face fell. "Yes, it's a tragedy. I can't imagine what happened. I know one thing though. Rose didn't do it."

"I don't believe she did either," Alfred said. "I mean, she's getting on there in age, and I'm sure her mind's not as sharp as it used to be. Perhaps this is a case of someone with early dementia making a simple mistake."

"My grandmother's mind is as good today as it was twenty years ago," Melly said with a frown.

He shrugged. I looked him over. About Sue's age or perhaps a few years younger, Alfred sat in the chair beside the bed, his hand resting on Sue's thigh. Like her, he wore dark jeans and a t-shirt, his with "Got Milk?" emblazoned on the front.

"Whoever put the Xylitol in Grannie's punch knew what they were doing," Melly said with a growl. "As for Grannie's memory, I was with her when her doctor did a full dementia screening. She does it every year for older patients. But Grannie passed without one hitch."

"She's as sharp as she was when we were in high school," Sue said. "Detective Carter will find out who did it and they'll pay."

Was Alfred involved? It was hard to say.

Why were they keeping their marriage hidden?

Because I knew our time was limited, I asked them a few basic questions, determining they'd arrived as Grannie was about to go to the bathroom. Sue helped Grannie Rose into the stall and waited a moment to make sure she didn't need help before coming back out into the main room. The bathroom was located in the hallway between the church and the function room.

The nurse bustled in while I was quizzing them. She gathered Sue's belongings and put them in a plastic bag emblazoned with the hospital's logo.

"I love that punch," Sue said wistfully. "It's one of the few good things Rose can do."

Melly huffed.

"What?" Sue said with a low laugh. "Your grandmother's mittens are not as wonderful as she'd like everyone to believe."

"They're amazing," Melly said, her gaze meeting mine. "You know that."

"Well, that's what the town says, so I guess it must be true, right?" Sue's laugh held a harsh edge. "As for the punch, in that, she excels." Her gaze flicked to Melly. "You have the recipe. You should share it with me sometime."

"You know Grannie doesn't want anyone else knowing her secret ingredients," Melly said.

"One day, I'll figure it out." Sue's smile contained no humor. "I often drink three or four glasses of it through the evening. I was thirsty because this one . . ." She laid her hand on Alfred's and squeezed. "This man thought it would be fun to hike one of the trails through the woods on the edge of town. Did you know the Mystic Harbor Hiking Society has been working in the forest behind the park? They've cleared three new trails for walking, and one of them is over four miles long. Somehow, Alfred and I ended up on that one. I was so tired, hungry, and thirsty when we finished, but by then, it was almost time to leave for the church social, so we just grabbed our potluck offering and scooted to the church."

"Where you drank the punch," I said.

"Tainted punch," Alfred said with a scowl. His worried gaze met Sue's. "Her kidney function took a solid hit. I hope Detective Carter arrests the correct person soon, because I'd like to have a word with them. They hurt my girlfriend, and I want to see them pay."

"I'm sorry about your kidneys," Melly said.

Sue shrugged. "Fate sure is determined to kill me early."

Melly gasped. "What do you mean?"

"My kidneys aren't recovering from this as much as I'd like."

"You can do dialysis," Alfred said softly, wringing his hands on his lap.

"I don't want to. I told you that already." Sue's gaze met mine. "My dad was on dialysis. He was a diabetic, which fortunately, I'm not. His kidneys failed, and he did dialysis for three years while waiting and hoping for a kidney transplant. I gave him one of mine, but his body rejected it. Can you imagine that? We were a perfect match, and it still wasn't enough." Her fingertip traced along the seam of the bed spread. "I don't have a spare kidney any longer. It's ironic that the one I still have has decided it's had enough. But I won't do dialysis. It wore my dad out each time, and I'm not going to go through that as well. I'm old. If I die now, it's my time, and I accept that."

The nurse gave me an odd look but didn't say anything.

Alfred stood and rounded the bed. "Well, *I* don't accept it." He grabbed the papers, folded them, and stuffed them into the manilla envelope lying beneath them marked with Sterling Life and Indemnity. "I'm going to do all I can to talk you into considering dialysis." After tucking the envelope into a tote bag sitting on the floor, he straightened and looked toward Melly. "Speak with Rose, will you? See if she can talk to Sue."

"I'm right here, Alfred." An edge had crept back into Sue's voice. "Rose knows how I feel already."

The nurse strode closer to the bed. "Are you about ready to leave, Sue?"

"I believe so," she said. A woman wearing bright pink scrubs brought a wheelchair into the room. "There's my ride now." She looked up at me. "Do you have any more questions, Elrik?"

"Not right now."

"Well, if you do," she rattled off a phone number, and I noted it in my mind, "feel free to call." Her smile fell on Melly. "Thank you so much for stopping by, sweetie. I appreciate it. Say hi to your grannie for me. Tell her I'll stop by her place for coffee soon."

Melly gave Sue a kiss on the cheek. "I will. Take care. Let me know when you're coming for coffee so I can join you."

"I will, sweetie. I will."

We left and went out to my truck.

"Poor Sue," Melly said with a sigh. "It sounds like she's going to die." Her teary gaze met mine. "She and Grannie have been friends forever. I feel like she's my second grandmother. But I do understand why she feels that way about dialysis. I remember her mentioning more than once how tough it was for her father, how she would never want to do it herself. I guess we have to respect that, since this is how she wants to live her life." She buckled and stared through the windshield, sighing.

"I saw you trying to get a peek at the paperwork she signed. Did you see what it was?"

"I did," I said grimly.

Melly shot a frown my way. "You sound concerned."

"That paperwork she signed? It changed her life insurance policy beneficiary to Alfred."

11

MELLY

"Alfred has a motive and the means to commit the crime," I said as Elrik drove his truck from the hospital parking lot and into town.

"I'll notify Detective Carter of what we'd discovered and overheard." Elrik pulled his vehicle into the lot across the street from Creature Cones and shut off the engine. "But this doesn't mean he dumped the Xylitol in Grannie's punch. Others were there that evening. This could be a coincidence."

I stared through the windshield, my face hot and my hands flexing into fists on my lap. "Why haven't they announced they got married? That's what I want to know. Grannie must not know about it. You'd think Sue would've told her. They're best friends."

"Ask her."

"I plan to."

We got out of the truck and crossed the road.

"Did you discover anything online?" I asked, wondering what surprises he might've unearthed about my grandmother's other friends. You could live your entire life in a community and think you knew everything about everyone, only to have something creep up behind you and bite you on the butt.

"A few things, though nothing worth mentioning yet," he said. "I'll look some more tonight." He opened the door to the ice cream shop for me, and we stepped inside, finding only Carla there, sitting at one of the tables, scrolling on her phone.

She sprung up as we stepped into the shop. "There you are."

"Has it been busy?" It wasn't right now, but this must be a lull.

"It was one customer after another for about an hour after you left, but it suddenly slowed right down to nothing."

This was odd for a sunny midday, but I was sure the place would be swarming with customers soon.

"Would you believe only one person has been in for ice cream in the past hour?" Carla said.

"That *is* weird." I turned to stare out the plate glass window. Maybe there was a fair outside of town and that had drawn everyone away. Or they were all at the beach. Eating at restaurants. Avoiding ice cream for some strange reason.

Elrik shot me a frown.

Carla joined me at the window. "I don't get it either. I thought I'd be run ragged while you were gone."

"I'm sorry we took so long."

Carla shrugged. "I don't mind. It's my job."

"Something came up with Elrik's truck," I said. "And

then we went to the hospital to see Sue before she was discharged."

"How's she doing?"

"You should give her a call or go see her." It wasn't my place to discuss her health and her need for dialysis, but I was sure Sue would mention it at the next church social —assuming they held one again. They might decide to cancel them for the foreseeable future.

It also wasn't my place to discuss Carla kissing Alfred.

"I'll give her a few days and then do that." She flashed me a smile, and I didn't get the impression she was uncomfortable about the idea of visiting the girlfriend of the man she'd kissed.

"Would you like to take a break?" I asked. "I owe you."

"Sure. I want to walk down Main Street and feel the salty breeze in my hair." She dimpled her smile Elrik's way. "Would you like to walk with me? You must have more questions."

"I'm afraid I can't." His gaze sought mine. "I need to go to the office and take care of a few things. I'll see you later?"

"Do you want to get together after I close at four?" I didn't need to remind him of the time. I'd mentioned it yesterday, and he wasn't the type to forget. But for some reason, I wanted to make it plain to Carla that Elrik was taken. Sort of. Was that what it meant when a guy declared he was your fated mate?

"I can come by when you close." He shot me another smile that faded quickly. After giving Carla a curt nod, he left.

She stared after him and sighed. "Did you work on

getting a ring on your finger while you were gone?" She ran her hand through the sunlight beaming in through the big window, making her enormous diamond sparkle.

"We're just friends."

"A friend who's coming by the moment you close down this place?" Her low laugh rang out. "I assume you're going to . . . I don't know. Stroll through town. Make him a home-cooked meal. They do say the way to a man's heart is through his stomach."

"Is that how you hooked Walter?"

"He did enjoy my hot crossed buns." She winked, but the light dropped away from her eyes. "Every time I make them, I think of him."

I rubbed her arm. "I'm sorry."

After nodding, she went out to the tiny room behind the main part of the shop to grab her purse, returning to exit out the front door. "I won't be long. I'll loop around Main Street and come back to help. I'm sure we'll be busy by then."

"I bet we will."

The bell jangled as she opened the door, and I followed her out onto the sidewalk. Maybe I should set up a table and give out samples. That was how I'd drawn in customers when I first opened.

"There you are." Estadore, the griffin realtor who owned Griffin Grove Real Estate Group hurried down the sidewalk, his lion's mane ruffling in the breeze and his tail swishing behind him. He was one of three griffins in town, though they weren't related, and he was a sweetie. He'd stopped by the hospital after Grannie broke her hip to bring her flowers.

"Hello," I said, hoping he was here for ice cream.

However, he stopped beside Carla, only giving me a nod.

"Wonderful news," he said to Carla. "We've got an offer on the place in Florida."

"Ahh!" Carla's bright gaze met mine before she turned back to Estadore.

I hadn't realized she'd put the Florida place up for sale, but I wasn't surprised. She hadn't gone there in years. She said her heart wasn't in it without Walter. I could swear she'd mentioned that she was thinking of renting it, though maybe I'd misheard. While a real estate agency could handle short- and even long-term rentals, things got broken or damaged. She'd shown me pictures, and the house was full of gorgeous antiques. I couldn't imagine renting it as it was.

To give them privacy, I walked over to the window boxes and started grooming the annuals I'd planted there this spring. I wasn't trying to listen in, but the wind caught their words and sent them in my direction.

"How much is the offer?" Carla asked with excitement.

He named a price that made my eyeballs pop.

Her growl rumbled my way. "That's not enough. I told you I needed a certain amount. The second mortgage . . ." She glanced in my direction.

When I saw how pink her face was, I opened the door and went inside.

This time, I did snoop on purpose. I crept over to the open window, close to where they stood.

Second mortgage? Carla had inherited a lot of money

—so she'd bragged around town multiple times. Why would she need to borrow money against the property?

"This price will cover both the first and second mortgage," Estadore said.

"I want more. I need it." Desperation came through in Carla's hissed voice. "Counteroffer." She named a figure that made my eyes widen even farther. "I won't take less than that."

"I thought you wanted to wash your hands of the properties."

Properties with an S?

"I do, but . . ." She lowered her voice.

I leaned against the wall beside the window, straining to hear their every word.

"You were able to liquidate the belongings?" she said.

"Yes, I got quite a bit for them at auction." He named a number that made my heart flip over. "I mailed the cashier's check, and you deposited it."

"Yes, I did. Sorry. I forgot. It was barely enough to cover my current expenses. Contrary to popular belief, my husband didn't . . ."

What expenses? Shouldn't everything be covered by the wealth Walter had left her in his will?

"I'm sorry you're having financial difficulties," Estadore said. "I'm doing all I can to help. But the market is horrible in Florida right now. Hurricanes, politics, and the insurance fiasco are making everyone eager to sell. I think this offer is solid, and you should seriously consider taking it."

"I can't accept it. What's left after paying off Walter's loans will barely cover three payments on my place here."

Wait. Walter took out loans on both properties? He'd been dead for ten years. He'd supposedly left Carla the two homes, plus more money than she could spend in a lifetime. If that was the case, and he'd, for some reason, taken out loans on both of the properties, why hadn't she used the money she inherited to pay them off years ago?

"I'm truly sorry," he said. "As for your home here, we're seeing a lot more interest. I think we'll have a solid offer soon."

She was selling the house on the water as well?

"I have three groups coming later this week to take a look, and one of them is particularly eager," Estadore added. "Your home here on the Cape is exactly what they've been looking for."

"And the auction for the furnishings?"

"All arranged."

"You said you'd be discreet. I don't want anyone learning about my . . . difficulties."

"This company is impeccable. No one in this community will know a thing."

Except me. She was hawking all her belongings, selling the properties Walter had left her. What would she offer for sale next—the very large diamond engagement ring Walter had given her?

I felt bad for her. Despite looking like she was a gold digger to almost everyone in town, I knew she wasn't. She'd loved Walter. I'd seen that in their every interaction. Now it appeared he'd left her a bunch of debt.

She'd had ten years to figure this out. Why wait until now to sell?

Perhaps she'd used what little money he left her to

cover the payments on both loans. But she'd known that would run out. How did she expect to make payments on the debt after that? She worked part time for me, and while I paid above minimum wage, she wasn't making enough to cover the rent on an apartment in town, let alone interest payments on two mortgaged waterfront properties.

"I'll reach out once the three have looked at your property here in town," he said.

"Thanks."

As Estadore left, I walked over to the counter and casually leaned against it.

Carla crossed the street and hurried down the sidewalk, taking her walk.

With no customers and them gone, I went back outside and sat on one of the pretty iron chairs, giving Elrik a call. I filled him in on what I'd overheard, though I wasn't sure any of the information played a role in what happened at the church social.

"It's interesting that you overheard all this," Elrik said. "I was just doing a deep dive into Carla and Walter online. Walter *was* wealthy at one time, but a divorce with a different, though also very young woman left him short on cash. He was able to hold onto the properties in Florida and here in town, but to do so, he had to sell most of his shares in his business. When he married Carla, there wasn't much left but the properties. He mortgaged both homes not only to buy her the huge ring she's wearing, but to give her the impression he had endless wealth."

"Wow," I said. "You found all that online?"

"With some snooping."

"When I look online, all that comes up is porn."

His low laugh rang out. "Do you click on it?"

"And risk picking up a computer virus? Never."

"Wise."

I scrunched my face. "That's me. Hopefully, I'm wise enough to discover who wants to put my grandmother in jail. Carla hasn't shared any of this with me, not that she'd have to, though she must know I'd understand."

"If she can't find buyers fast, she'll lose both places to the bank. Over the past ten years since Walter's death, she's continued to live the lifestyle he promised her. She's attended Broadway shows. I saw pictures of that online. Other images showed her coming out of highly exclusive restaurants and making purchases at Tiffany's."

"You'd think she'd remember how to be frugal."

He grunted in agreement. "Without money coming in, my assumption is she's had to dip into what Walter had left in investments. She's no longer even a minor shareholder in his business, so she must've sold those shares years ago. She's a month late on the second mortgage he took out on the Florida place, so I can see why she's eager to sell."

"For the right price. I doubt she wants to lose money on the sale." Poor Carla. She must be eager to get rid of all that debt. Yet why continue living a lifestyle she couldn't afford?

"She's not making much at Creature Cones," I said. "She implied to me this job was something fun to do to get out of the house, that she was tired of sitting on the deck overlooking the water and reading books. I could give her a raise and offer her more hours, but I doubt that'll make much difference. I wonder if she has other assets she can sell."

"I suspect not if she's selling both properties."

"That's one thing I don't understand. After ten years of making payments, she should've taken care of a good portion of the debt. She should have equity in the properties."

"Not if you only pay the interest on the loans," he said.

"I assume you discovered that online as well. How was such a thing allowed?"

"Walter's brother was a banker. He did the deal himself."

"Wow. I imagine he got in trouble for that."

"He doesn't appear to have suffered. He has a huge place on Long Island. A young wife."

"It runs in the family. Maybe he'll help Carla out." She should ask him.

"I doubt he will. According to what I discovered online, he was opposed to their marriage."

"I was a teenager when they got married." I smiled at the memory. "She asked me to be her junior bridesmaid. Grannie helped me pick out a dress, and I got to straighten her long train when she stood at the altar beside Walter. You could be right, however. I might've seen things with a dreamy eye back then. Walter was old. No denying that. But he was a nice guy, and he doted on Carla. She seemed to feel the same, and I took it at face value."

"She may have loved him. It wouldn't be the first time."

"I always thought she did. I'm sure on the surface, it looked like she didn't. He was so much older than her. Many in town thought she was only after his wealth."

Supposed wealth. If she was, her eyes had been opened after he died. "For what it's worth, she seemed to care for him. They were happy."

"It's really hard to tell with something like that."

"Does any of this tie Carla to the Xylitol?" I was confident Alfred had done it, but maybe Elrik was looking at this from an angle I hadn't seen.

"I'm not sure. I'm still following a few leads."

"Well, keep me informed."

"I will."

I hung up and stood, realizing that I'd had no customers for longer than I could remember on a warm summer day.

A human couple with two small children were walking my way.

"Half price sale," I said cheerfully. "Two cones for the price of one."

They stopped and while the kids hopped around in excitement, the parents stared at me in horror.

"That's the place we read about online. Johnny. Janie. Come with me." The woman jutted out her hands to her children, and once they'd latched on, the family pivoted and hurried down the walkway in the opposite direction.

Read about online? My reviews were excellent. I hadn't even picked up a one-star troll yet, though I expected it would happen one of these days.

With fear jarring through me, I hurried inside and pulled my phone out of my back pocket. I scrolled to the Mystic Harbor website, the one where my five-star average consistently winked. Creature Cones had even been featured at the top of the "places to try" section on our town's home page.

My business now had a one-point-six review average.

Days ago, my business had been rated four point nine with thousands of raving reviews. Now, my ice cream shop had over two thousand new one-star ratings.

Many of the reviews warned people not to go anywhere near Creature Cones.

Unless they wanted to be poisoned.

12

ELRIK

My phone rang. Melly again.

I'd stalled with the investigation and had planned to go through a case Monsters, PI had just taken on, one involving a local selkie clan and the theft of the king's and queen's skins when they came to shore for dinner. We were sure it was a prank. Kids sometimes didn't think before doing things like that. But we were also determined to track down their skins and return them.

"Hello?" I said with a smile. "Let me guess," I joked. "You were scrolling through porn, and you *had* to reach out to me."

"Elrik!"

At Melly's frantic cry, I bolted to my feet, peering around as if a threat to her loomed inside my office. "What's wrong?"

"Someone's trolling my business." Her voice choked off with a sob. "I've got a troll. A very mean troll."

Troll?

Despite being a monster myself, I had only met one troll in my life, a hulking, ten-foot-tall dude with mottled green skin and wiry black hair sticking out in all directions. From what I'd read online, his physical appearance was the norm for his species. I'd met him during one of my jobs when he'd volunteered to help us find a lost three-year-old girl, who thankfully was found and returned to her family.

The troll's bulbous nose sat above a wide mouth filled with jagged teeth, but the little girl had run right to him when we appeared. He'd scooped her up and cradled her in his enormous green arms, telling her over and over again that she was safe.

Unfortunately, I'd lost touch with him not long after that.

"I'll be right over," I told Melly. Creature Cones was only a few doors down, and I strode inside within moments.

She locked the door behind me and turned the sign on the door to Closed before taking my hand and tugging me around the counter and into the back room. She sat at a table and wrung her hands on her lap while I leaned against the counter of the small kitchen area. A door on my left was labeled Freezer, and through the open doorway on the right, I spied a hallway and a set of stairs leading up. Grannie had rented an apartment up there at one time. No one was living there at the moment.

"Someone's trying to ruin my business." Melly scrolled into her phone and handed it to me. "Look at this. Thousands of bad reviews for Creature Cones. None of them make sense. They're saying I'm poisoning people."

"What?" I flipped through the comments, most coming from Anonymous, something the site must allow for confidentiality.

"I don't understand." Melly's eyes shimmered with tears. "But this has to be related to the social club poisoning."

"I can't imagine how."

"They left a warning on your truck. Now this. I think someone will do almost anything to make us stop investigating. At this point, it wouldn't surprise me to discover that Anonymous is the one who dumped Xylitol into Grannie's punch."

Frowning, I handed her phone back to her, and she laid it on the table. "This could be a bunch of random trolls. You know how mean people can be, how some like to gather together with a few friends and gang up on a business. Have you received odd emails from anyone?"

"Why would someone like that email me?"

"It's not unheard of for people like that to one-star a business and then ask for money to remove the bad reviews."

"Extortion?"

"Sadly, yes."

She quickly scrolled into her email before shaking her head. "No new email other than one from someone eager to sell me something to increase my penis size."

Under any other circumstances, I'd make a joke about that, but this was serious business.

"No email demanding money," she added, laying her

phone back on the small table next to her chair. She heaved a sigh. Settling in the chair, she tipped her head back and closed her eyes. "I don't know what to do about this. I'll reach out to the group who runs the website to see if they're willing to delete the ratings. Other than a few mentioning poisonings, none left real reviews. Surely, they won't allow random ratings like that to remain. This could ruin me."

Carla opened the back door and stepped inside, her gaze flicking to me before landing Melly. "Hey, did you know the front door is locked? I couldn't get in."

Melly handed her phone to Carla. "We've got a problem."

Carla's eyes widened as she read. "What is this? How dare they?"

"I'm worried the two things are connected," Melly said.

"You think someone found out what happened at the social function and decided our ice cream must be poisoned as well?" Carla bit down hard on her lower lip, her brow scrunching. "It makes no sense. Everyone knows your grandmother would never do anything like that. Not unless she was getting forgetful and added too much Xylitol by mistake."

"She doesn't put any Xylitol in her punch," Melly snapped, taking the phone back and sliding it into her pocket. "The recipe doesn't call for that. It's an old recipe from before Xylitol was even created."

"You'd know," Carla said. "You're the sole person she's share the recipe with. You made the punch while she was in rehab and since she was released. Other than the most recent punch, that is." She sat at the small table opposite Melly. "I've got a friend who runs a PR firm in Boston. Would you like me to reach out to her to see if she has any suggestions? Unless you want to handle this yourself."

"That would be wonderful." Melly rubbed her face with both hands. "Thanks."

"We've closed for the day, I take it. No wonder we weren't seeing any customers earlier. This is horrible." Carla rose and started pacing inside the tiny kitchen. "We need to open the shop soon. I need this . . ." Pausing, she sucked in a breath and released it, her hands fisting, then opening at her sides. Spinning, she faced us. "I'm going to go take a quick walk on the beach. That'll clear my head and help me come up with some ideas to help you."

"Actually, why don't you take the rest of the day off?" Melly said. "We won't open again today. When you get here in the morning, we'll brainstorm."

Carla strode over to Melly and braced her shoulders, staring into her eyes. "No one's going to ruin this business. We're going to fix this."

"Thank you."

Bending closer, Carla gave Melly a long hug. "I just don't get it. You work hard. You've done all you can to make this business a success. People suck."

"You're right," Melly said. "They do."

Carla straightened. "I'll call you if I think of anything, and I'll let you know what my friend says. I'm sure she has some suggestions."

"I'm more than willing to pay her if she has some ideas that can fix this."

"Let me see what she says." Carla's smile came out grim. "She owes me, and it's time for me to call in that favor." She grabbed her purse and left through the back door.

Melly's gaze met mine. "Why would anyone do something like this?"

"I don't know, but we're going to find out."

Her phone pinged with an incoming text, and she lifted the phone and read.

"Like those ratings? Stop investigating or it'll get worse," she read dully, tilting the screen my way. "It *is* related. Why is someone so determined to ruin Grannie Rose?"

"Let me see." I wrote down the number and looked it up online, finding nothing. "I'm sure they used a burner phone. No one would send a threatening text message with their own line."

"I feel like we're no closer to solving this crime than we were when we started." Utter defeat filled Melly's voice.

I hated seeing her feeling like this. How could I give her hope? "Detective Carter was intrigued by the information about Sue and Alfred. He was going to question them both."

"Alfred has a motive. My grandmother does not."

Tugging her up from the chair, I held her, wishing I could give her comfort in some way. "It hasn't been long. This may take time."

"I know." She leaned back in my arms. "Thank you for helping, for being here for me."

“We’re going to keep investigating. We’re not giving up.”

“We’ll have to be more careful, or they could do something more serious than cut your radiator hoses or ruin my business.”

“That’s why we’re going to remain alert. If someone tries something, we’ll catch them.”

“They’ve been good at hiding the evidence so far.”

“They’ll make a mistake.” I tilted her chin and gave her a quick kiss before hugging her again. I spoke against her hair. “They always do, and then we’ll catch them.”

13

MELLY

The next evening, the chicken was sitting on the top of the stove until it cooled enough for me to cut, and I was finishing making the gravy, when someone knocked on the back kitchen door.

We hadn't made any progress in the investigation yet because Elrik had been needed on another case that he'd thankfully solved. Something about selkie skins and a king and a queen, a thing I couldn't quite fathom. Although, I didn't know why I was surprised. With monsters roaming the land, why hadn't it occurred to me that there were an equal number of them living deep in the sea?

"Elrik's here," Grannie Rose said with a big grin. She'd sat at the kitchen table to "supervise" the meal preparation, though she'd mostly drank tea and worked on another mitten. "I'm so looking forward to this evening."

I felt bad. I was too busy to take her to many places,

which meant she barely got out. A physical therapist came twice a week, and my grandmother was getting stronger. If she could get rid of the walker, she might be able to drive herself again. Once we'd cleared her name —and I was determined that we would—she could get back to the active social life she'd had before her fall.

Striding over to the side entrance, I opened the door.

Elrik bustled inside, juggling a bottle of wine, flowers, and two small heart-shaped boxes of chocolate.

"Ohh," Grannie exclaimed, rising from her chair. "What do you have there, my fine-looking ice lord?"

He juggled the items, handing me the wine, his sultry smile sinking through my skin in the nicest way. "For us to share tonight."

"Not me," Grannie Rose said. "I can't take that with my rat poison."

His eyebrows lifted. "Rat poison?"

"I'm on a blood thinner to prevent clots in my legs," she said. "They use it as rat poison, didn't you know? The rats eat a lot of it and well . . ."

I winced.

She grinned. "They bleed to death."

"Ugh. Grannie," I said.

"I did not know that." Elrik's sparkling eyes met mine. "Melly and I will share the wine, then. It's a great year. I think you'll like it."

"Thank you for bringing it." I held up the bottle, squinting at the label. "A merlot, my favorite."

"Good." His face darkened, and he jutted out his hand holding one of two bouquets of flowers. "For a lovely lady."

Before I could say anything, he was holding out the second bouquet to Grannie. "And this is for the second lovely lady in the room."

"Do you know how long it's been since someone gave me flowers?" Grannie asked, holding them like she would a baby, gazing down at them with complete joy. "Too long."

"You need more flowers in your life." Elrik held out one of the boxes of chocolate toward her. "Also for you. I hope you can still eat chocolate despite being on a blood thinner."

"I can. Yum." She took the box and laid it on the table, studying the contents. "Nuts! I love chocolate covered nuts the best. Not those gooey hunks of nougat some boxes come with."

"I'm so glad I got the right ones." Elrik sent me a smile. "What about you? Do you enjoy chocolate covered nuts?" He held the other box toward me.

There was nothing sexy in his question but heat still flared through me.

"I love chocolate, thank you." He was sweet to think of us this way, but that was Elrik. "Dinner will be ready in a few minutes. If you want, you and Grannie can go into the living room to wait. I'll dish up and let you know when it's time to eat, which we'll do in the dining room."

He lifted his chin, sniffing. "Whatever you've made smells amazing."

"Roasted chicken, mashed potatoes with gravy, and green beans. I made a cake for dessert." I'd made it the second I got home from work, which was so early even Grannie remarked on it. The PR person had taken on the challenge, but we'd seen no results yet, which meant we didn't have one single customer. Discouraged, I'd closed and sent Carla home—though I'd pay her for her time. It wasn't her fault business was creeping along slower than the pace of a glacier.

When Grannie asked why I came home mid-afternoon, I told her I'd closed up early to give myself time to make a nice meal for her and Elrik. I didn't want to worry her. She'd feel responsible for the negative reviews even though she'd done nothing wrong.

"What can I do to help?" he asked.

"Everything's almost ready, so go sit with Grannie. I don't mind putting things in serving dishes and bringing them into the dining room."

"I think we can help her with that, don't you, Elrik?" Grannie asked. After setting aside her knitting, she used her walker to go over to the counter. "I'll bring the potatoes in if you grab the beans."

When she started to lift the platter, he took it from her. "Let me carry both."

She cocked her head to look up at him. "You're sure?"

"Completely sure."

"Then I'll tell you where you can put them." She followed him toward the dining room, her walker clunking on the hardwood floor.

I put the flowers in vases and placed them on the dining room table for us to enjoy. I returned to the kitchen and opened the wine, poured two glasses, and then started slicing the chicken. When Elrik returned, I had him ladle the gravy into the server and take that into the dining room as well. He took our glasses of wine, plus juice for Grannie, served in a pretty glass.

When the chicken was ready, I joined them, placing the heaping platter on the dining room table.

It hadn't been that long since Grannie entertained people here. The table could easily support ten. Now the three of us would sit on one end.

"Take the head of the table," Grannie told Elrik. "My deceased husband used to sit there. I think that position holds the most respect, don't you?"

"Then you should take it," he told her.

"Nah. I'm a peanut. I'll settle on one side."

I helped her sit in her chair and move it close to the table, then placed her walker near the wall. Rounding the table, I sat opposite her with Elrik, who was still standing, on my left side.

Once we'd both settled in our seats, I lifted the platter of chicken and offered it to him, grinning at the big portion he took.

We passed the food around and once we'd served everything, we dug in.

"The chicken's cooked to perfection," Grannie said, clicking her dentures. "I taught you well."

"You did." Her praise was a little thing, but she wasn't one to do more than pat me on the back every now and then. I'd always assumed her lack of physical touch was due to her upbringing, but it made me sad. My mom hadn't given out many hugs either, come to think of it. As for my dad, he'd bailed before he could hold me even once.

But I didn't want to feel upset about that tonight. My

life was going very well. I could find pride for my accomplishments within myself. I didn't need anyone else to hand that to me.

"The meal is wonderful," Elrik said. "Everything. Your gravy is particularly amazing."

My face grew hot. "Thank you."

"See?" Grannie said slyly. "The way to a male's heart is through his stomach."

I chuckled. "Carla seems to think so too."

"Did she say that?" Her lips twisted, and the humor left her eyes. "She wouldn't know. From what I heard, she never cooked a single meal for Walter."

"She said he enjoyed her hot crossed buns."

"That she bought from a bakery."

Really? "Maybe they enjoyed going out to eat."

"I doubt it. He started making plans to divorce her within a few weeks of the wedding."

I gaped at her. "I can't believe that. They were in love." I swallowed my bite of chicken that clawed its way down.

Grannie grunted. "That woman never loved anyone but herself."

"Grannie Rose. Why am I hearing all of this now? You always spoke well of her. You had her babysit me."

"She was good at watching a twelve-year-old child; I'll give her that, but she wasn't a good wife to Walter. Did you know he and I had talked about marrying at one time? We'd dated for almost a year when she lured him away."

My head was spinning. What alternate reality had I suddenly stumbled into? "You and Walter . . ."

"Did you think I had him over to dinner all those

times because I was a nice person? He was courting me, and I was letting him do so." She huffed. "I should've moved on him faster, though. Then things might've worked out between us."

I was so stunned I could barely compose and speak my thoughts. "You're the one who encouraged me to hire her at Creature Cones."

Elrik watched our conversation, his head snapping from one of us to the other like this was a prize-winning tennis match.

"I felt bad for her after he died." Her cackle rang out. "He got the last laugh, though, now didn't he? He left her nothing. Well, some shares of stock in his company that I'm sure she sold and then squandered the money within a few years."

"He left her two gorgeous homes."

Her snide smile grew wider. "Gorgeous homes that came with debt."

"Grannie." I shook my head, lowering my fork to my plate and leaving it there. I'd lost my appetite. "Give me a second to process this."

Her smile slipped. "Before he died, he told me she threatened him." Shadows swirled in her hazel eyes.

My hands trembled on my lap. "Excuse me?"

"She told him if he didn't make right by her, she'd tell the world he was having financial difficulties. If nothing else, Walter had his pride." Something Grannie valued above almost everything else.

"He had enough left for her to live a high-class life for the past ten years," Elrik pointed out. Was he taking notes about all this? We should be asking Grannie for the dirt on each person who attended the church social, not spend our time snooping online. Grannie was a gold mine of information.

"He had enough to leave her—to shut up her threats—because I helped him," Grannie said. "He'd had a rough go of it. Business issues. But he was doing better after he sold most of the shares in his company to me. He gave me a sweet deal. Boy, was Clara mad when she found out. I offloaded them a few years ago. Hazel took care of that for me, naturally."

"Hazel, the pole dance instructor?" Elrik asked.

"She worked on the stock market before she retired," Grannie said. "She's been my investment counselor for years."

Hazel had managed the small amount of money my dad left when he died, but I hadn't realized she'd managed Grannie's finances, let alone that Grannie had much money to invest.

"When did you sell the shares in his company?" I asked.

"Five months ago."

"Why so recently?"

"Walter's brother was in town. He wants to buy Walter's place on the water, and he made Carla a reasonable offer. She turned him down, haughty thing that she is. She swore at him, told him Walter hated him, which might've been true at one time. Walter never spoke well of his brother."

I still couldn't believe what I was hearing, and it was clear from Elrik's lifted eyebrows that he was as surprised as me.

"Walter's brother got even, however," Grannie Rose said. "He told her *why* Walter left her nearly nothing." Her sly grin rose. "Walter loved me. He told me that on his deathbed. And that's why he changed his will at the last minute, leaving almost everything to me."

14

ELRIK

"Walter and Carla remained married until he died four years after the wedding," Melly said in a breathy voice. It was clear she was shocked by what she was learning. So was I. Carla was moving to the top of our suspect list.

"In addition to threatening to tell everyone about his financial difficulties," Grannie said, "she threatened to tell everyone we were having an affair. Can you believe that? She even said she'd name me in the divorce papers. He gave up and remained with her." Her gaze fell to her plate. "He was a sweet man for protecting my reputation in this community. You know a scandal like that would spread across town like a wildfire."

"Yes." Melly blinked slowly. "You instilled that need to avoid drawing attention into me."

Grannie reached across the table and tapped Melly's hand lying beside her plate. "And I did a very good job with that. You have never given me a reason to be concerned. You have yet to stay late at a man's house. You did well in school. You excelled in college and even while you were there, you didn't give anything to the town's gossips. You moved back to town where you have solid roots, your business is doing well and is respectable, and you're helping me. Everyone sees this. They can tell how wonderful you are."

"Yes." Her face paling, Melly swallowed hard. "I won't do anything to disappoint you."

As she placed her hand on her lap, Grannie Rose scoffed. "Unlike your father. That cursed man shirked his responsibilities and took off." Her rheumy gaze met mine. "Walter's company grew under his brother's management, so when he came to me, eager to buy the shares, I gave him a good deal. Hazel advised me, naturally. She always looks out for my bottom line."

"I didn't realize you had much money," Melly said.

"I don't flaunt it, another thing those in town might frown upon," Grannie said smugly. She pushed her empty plate away. "I believe I'd like to wait for cake, if that's alright. I'm quite full already."

Melly swallowed again. "Of course. I don't believe I have any appetite for cake myself."

"Take your wine to the backyard." Grannie pushed back her chair and rose. She latched onto her walker and started toward the living room. "I want to watch my shows on TV. Last week, that sweet young detective was left in a bind. A cliffhanger, they call it. Don't they realize that an old person like me might not live long enough to find out what happens next?" She left the dining room.

"I'll clear the table." Melly shot me a shocked look.

"You can take our wine outside if you want, and I'll join you."

She looked so upset. How could I make this better for her? "I'll help."

It didn't take long to put the leftovers away and place the dishes in the dishwasher.

Outside, we settled on lounge chairs with only a murky light above the back door shedding beams across the well-maintained lawn. Grannie had chairs big enough for an orc. Ice lords weren't quite as large, but I appreciated furniture I could comfortably sit in, those that let me put my legs up without them sticking off the end.

We drank at least half our wine and watched the fireflies dance through the darkness before I finally spoke. "Your grandmother is a fountain of information."

"I'm still stunned," Melly said. "I can't believe it. Actually, I can, but you know what I mean. Grannie dating Walter. Him giving her a great deal on the stock in his company. And Carla! She really was a gold digger all this time."

"And obviously, a good actress."

"She has a motive for framing Grannie."

"You're right." I'd do some research later, but now we had two solid suspects, Carla and Alfred. "Spite can make people do horrible things."

15

MELLY

We finished the wine, speculating about what Grannie told us, but we didn't come up with anything new.

"After I finished the selkie case today, I did some more research into Alfred and Sue," Elrik said softly.

I doubted Grannie or anyone else was listening in. Her neighbors on one side were as old as her and went to bed early, and the ones on the opposite side had gone to Europe for the summer. Grannie was absorbed in her show.

"What did you discover?" Turning in my chair, I faced him. The moon had risen, and a billion stars shone down from the clear sky, the light making his blue skin glow in a magical way.

"Remember the insurance paperwork he had her sign?" he said. "I found the company online. They're local, and they manage all sorts of policies for the residents of Mystic Harbor and the surrounding community."

"Alfred urged her to sign the paperwork making him her beneficiary of a life insurance policy."

"Which means he's the only one who'll inherit."

"I haven't asked Grannie about their marriage yet. She was having physical therapy when I got here to make dinner, and she was tired after they were through. I told her to nap until it was closer to dinnertime."

"Maybe you'll have the chance tomorrow."

I was sure I would. I doubted I'd keep Creature Cones open if we had no customers. "The fact that Sue and Alfred are married is shocking, although I'll point out that it's relative to the stunning news Grannie just shared. But I don't see how their marriage or her naming him her beneficiary relates to someone poisoning Grannie's punch."

"From what I could gather by snooping in the town's private forum, Sue's policy could be worth millions."

"What?" I blinked up at him. "She was a kindergarten teacher before she retired. I wish they paid teachers more, but they don't. How could she have saved that much?"

"If she was frugal and consistently paid in for years, it's possible. Some of those policies will grow quickly if they're handled correctly."

"You discovered this on the Mystic Harbor forum? Although, it's private. I pretty much had to give a blood sample to be allowed access. I forget to go there most of the time, though I'll occasionally pop in to offer a discount coupon. I like to do things like that for the locals."

"It's a great marketing technique."

"Exactly. One person has the coupon and everyone else comes with them and pays full price. I started the business because I love ice cream and there wasn't a shop in town. When my dad died, we discovered he'd named me his heir." I held up my hand and released a rueful laugh. "Don't get too excited. He didn't have much. Grannie had Hazel invest my small inheritance."

"I'm still surprised she was a stockbroker, though I don't know why."

"It's not the first career you'd associate with a pole dancing instructor. When she was young, she had a promising career as a ballerina, but she suffered a terrible fall and had to quit. She told me once she took up pole dancing for stress relief. Working the stock exchange must be nerve wracking. When she retired, she decided to turn her hobby into a career and teach."

"Have you taken one of her classes?"

"I tried but kept falling. Not enough upper body strength, she said. She suggested I lift weights. I wasn't excited enough about it to do that."

"It might be fun to see you twirling around on a pole."

"I know most see pole dancing as a sexy thing, but it's hard work. It takes a lot of strength, coordination, and balance. I'm more of a walking-for-exercise kind of girl." I twirled my empty wine glass between my fingers. "Hazel managed the money my dad left me, and when I moved back to town, I used most of it to open Creature Cones. I don't have a lot left; even used equipment is expensive. Thankfully, I had some left. I'll use it if something breaks, I'm injured and can't work, or my business slumps, which it's currently doing."

How long would it be before I'd have to tap into my savings to keep Creature Cones open?

This had to get better. Please.

"Tell me what you discovered on the town forum," I said as a distraction from my worry.

"Alfred didn't outright name it, but someone was asking about Sterling in general, and he said they were a great company, that he had a friend who'd been paying into a policy for years and she'd saved millions. I realize I'm adding two to three and coming up with six, but I bet he meant Sue."

"They were friends for a long time before they married." Frowning, I tried to remember everything I could about him and their relationship. "She must've mentioned it to him. He talked her into getting married—"

"At the hospital, he said she was the one who peeked into the Elvis chapel and suggested they get married."

"People can be manipulated into doing things like that," I said. "How do you know it was Alfred posting on the forum about Sue's insurance policy?"

"His full name is Alfred Brightmore. Who else would use the screen name, Bright Alfie?"

"Ah." There was a good chance it was him, then. "Do you think Alfred put the Xylitol in the punch to ruin Sue's kidneys? As a pharmacist, he'd know it could be toxic if taken in large enough doses. Ironically, he called me awhile back and told me he was worried about Grannie. He thought she might have some early dementia. I shrugged it off, though I suspected he could be right. She was slowing down, forgetting things."

"Which could be dementia but also just a normal sign of aging. I forget things all the time myself."

"Me too. However, when she fell and broke her hip and was in the hospital, they did a full screening and said she's as sharp as a twenty-year-old. Not one hint of dementia yet. If Alfred had been planning this for some time, it would make sense for him to frame Grannie for the crime."

"He suggested something like that at the hospital."

"If Detective Carter could be convinced this was an accident and due to her supposed dementia, the case might be dismissed. The local DA is sharp but not one to lock someone up over an accident."

"They'd let it slide?"

"Oh, they'd handle it in a legal way, but everyone knows everyone here, and the DA's parents were good friends of Grannie's for years. They might suggest Grannie wanted to make a punch with less sugar this time and added Xylitol instead, but messed up and dumped in too much."

"Is anyone in the club a diabetic?"

"I don't know. It would be a simple thing to suggest and even simpler to believe. Grannie's case would be dismissed. Her rep here in town would suffer, and she'd be horrified and embarrassed. You know how much she values her standing in this community. But nothing more would come of it but a slap on her wrist and a stern warning to me to take better care of her."

"If Alfred's involved, he could be hoping Sue goes into full kidney failure and dies since she's refusing dialysis. He'd collect the insurance money and while some might be surprised to find out the two had secretly married, he'd probably have a ready excuse everyone would believe. If it even came out."

"Marrying her could be a ploy on his part to make sure no one else comes forward to claim the insurance payout."

"Does Sue have children or family?" he asked.

"She never married. I think she had a sister." I frowned, trying to remember. "I believe she died a few years ago. There are probably nieces or nephews, but a spouse would have a stronger claim, especially a spouse named as the beneficiary."

"You're right. No one would question him inheriting and if your grandmother is blamed for the Xylitol poisoning, no one would bother questioning Alfred. I read more about kidney failure online earlier. If her solitary kidney is as bad as she says, she probably won't live more than a few months."

My throat choked off with pain. I couldn't insist she do dialysis, not when she was making her wishes plain, but it hurt to think I'd soon lose the woman I considered a second grandmother.

"Someone needs to screenshot Bright Alfie's posts," I croaked.

"I already did, though they're not incriminating." Elrik took my hand and squeezed it. "I'm sorry. Sue's a sweet lady."

"About once a month, she brought me chocolate chip cookies. She knew I loved them, and Grannie never liked to bake. Grannie thought store-bought cookies were good enough, but they're not. They can't compete with those made with love."

"Maybe she'll change her mind."

"I doubt it, but I'm going to make sure she knows I love her and that I respect her wishes. That I'll miss her." Tears started trickling down my cheeks.

He scooped me up in his arms, settling me on his lap. "I'm sorry. It's always hard to lose someone you love." Sitting back on his recliner, he stretched out his legs.

"You haven't shared much about your family." I needed to stop going over this in my mind. One stressor had been piled on top of another, and I didn't want to be sobbing when I went back inside. That would upset Grannie, and she'd never been one to find sympathy for someone in tears. "You mentioned your brother. Do you have other siblings? I was an only child."

"I just have the one brother, Thad. He's older than me by eight years. We weren't close growing up. I think he resented having a new baby take his place."

"That's sad. I can't imagine how wonderful it would be to have a brother or sister to play with. To talk with as you grow up together. I had my mom who was often as stilted as Grannie, but she worked two jobs to support us after my dad left her. And when she got home, she was tired. She'd loved me; I knew that. But life was tough for us. When Mom died, Grannie took over my care. I'd stayed with her during school vacations and a few weeks each summer, but she wasn't used to having a child running around all the time. She encouraged me to have friends over, but that couldn't replace a sibling."

"I'm sorry."

"Why?"

"Because it sounds like you've had a sad life. I only want the best for you."

Was that him? I was beginning to suspect my life would be full of sunshine and happiness if we found a way to be together.

"Would you like to take a walk on the beach?" he asked. "You said you enjoy them."

"Sure. Let me go tell Grannie where we're going and make sure everything's set up for her to settle for the night."

We got up and he followed me inside.

"Is the evening over?" Grannie asked, setting aside her knitting and turning off the TV. Her show must've finished.

"We're going to take a walk on the beach," I said. "I wanted to say goodnight and make sure everything's ready in case I'm not back before you go to bed."

"You go on." Her smile rose as it slid from me to Elrik. "Have a nice walk. I love seeing you with a nice young male like Elrik. He's responsible. Respectful. And such a gentleman."

My face heated but I shot him a grin. "He is pretty sweet."

She nodded. "That he is."

I went to her bathroom and set out the things for her dentures, plus her mouthwash and the pills she took before bed each night. Since her vision wasn't what it used to be, I filled her medication set each week for her.

I got her a new water glass and placed it on the sink. Inside her bedroom, I turned down her blankets and laid out a clean nightie. I also shut off the lamp, leaving only the nightlight glowing in the corner, just the way she liked it.

When I stepped into the living room, I paused, watching Elrik sitting next to Grannie, admiring the mittens she'd already made. She must've pointed out the basket full of them sitting near her side table.

While he went through them, admiring the colors and the tight knit, she was outlining his hand on a piece of paper. She'd be crafting ice lord mittens within a week, and if I knew Grannie, she'd insist Katar come over so she could create a pattern for mittens that would fit an orc. He'd receive at least one pair for Christmas.

"I'm almost finished," Grannie Rose said, shooting me a smile. "There." She held up her pencil. "I appreciate it, Elrik."

"Of course." Before he stood, he leaned over and kissed her cheek. "I hope you sleep well." Rising, he went around the house, checking all the windows and the front door, making sure they were locked. He came over after to stand behind me, his warm hand on my shoulder.

"I can handle everything else, dear." Grannie held up a book entitled *Enticed by an Alien Warlord*. "I'm reading an alien romance tonight." She wiggled her eyebrows. "I can't wait to get to the steamy parts."

Once again, my grandmother surprised me. Did her friends know she read alien romance? I doubted it.

We left, making sure the back door was locked behind us.

"The beach isn't far." I waved in that direction. We were close enough we could hear the crash of the waves on the shore and smell the salty brine in the air. "It's quiet at night. All the tourists have gone to bed or settled inside their rentals, though you probably know that already."

"You heard I own a place on the water."

My cheeks heated. "Carla told me. I wasn't snooping."

"I don't mind even if you were snooping. Feel welcome to ask me anything. I'll happily share."

Holding hands, we walked down Grannie's driveway and turned right. The beach was only two blocks away.

"Granny can't see the ocean from her home, but she can smell it and feel it nearby," I said. "She used to tell me that the ocean was a part of her. It floats in her blood and has sunk into her bones. She can't bear to be too far away from it."

"Does she go there often?"

"I bring her at least weekly. We drive, of course, and she can't get down to the sea yet. We sit on a bench, though, and that's almost as good. At least she can put her toes in the sand. She hopes to walk there again soon. It's taken her a long time to recover from her fractured hip. The social worker at the hospital told me Grannie might not get strong enough to leave rehab, but she was determined. And with me next door to help out, she had options. She progressed well with rehab and came home sooner than most people her age do after a fall like that. She had surgery, and the spot still bothers her sometimes, but she refuses to let it slow her down—for very long, that is."

"She didn't use a walker before?"

"Nope. She was as spry as us."

The sidewalk emptied into a small parking lot for

residents of the buildings on either side, and we wove among the vehicles to reach the beach.

On the edge, I sat on the wooden bench and took off my shoes. "This is where we sit." I nudged my head toward the parking lot behind us. "They don't mind if I park there for a short time."

We left our shoes under the bench and strode out across the wide sandy beach, not stopping until we'd reached the water. Facing it, we remained in place, taking in the moon shimmering as it etched its way across the inky surface and the soft swish of the waves sliding toward us before retreating backward. A few people passed behind us, but the place was basically deserted.

"It's gorgeous," he said. "I didn't grow up near the ocean but like Grannie Rose, I feel like it's in my blood. I have a deck, and I love sitting there at night, listening to the waves and the call of the seagulls."

"I understand what she means about the ocean being in her blood. When I go inland, even for a short time, I miss it. It's like there's a thread between us. It stretches but it's always trying to tug me back to where I belong."

"I can feel that."

"The water's calmer here on the bay side of the Cape. The open Atlantic side has stiff cliffs and crashing waves. You can't swim there often. Too many riptides. But it's dramatic and furious, like that side is the wild sister who grew up doing whatever she pleased, and this side is the calmer, more sedate sibling who does what she's told."

"Which side calls to you most, Melly?"

"Oh, the Atlantic." I flashed him a smile and held out

my hand. “Let’s walk. The tide’s out, and we might find a few shells.”

He took my hand, and we strolled, him walking in the water with it gliding up to swirl around his ankles, me with it kissing my toes.

“Since you love the ocean, you must’ve enjoyed visiting your grandmother,” he said.

“Mom and I lived about forty minutes away, closer to Boston. When Mom sent me to stay with Grannie, I spent all day long here. I’d make a peanut butter and jelly sandwich, fill a water bottle, pack up the sand toys, and come to the beach.” We continued to stroll along the shore, kicking at the waves and pausing only to lift a pretty shell we’d toss into the sea.

“I grew up close enough to the glaciers that I could hike across them,” he said. “It’s a sharp contrast to this. Like the Atlantic side of the cape, the glaciers are the wilder brother where the green valleys are the tame brother.”

I grinned up at him. “And which do you feel closer to?”

He squeezed my hand. “Definitely the wild one.”

“I’ve seen pictures of deep crevasses and pristine blue and white ice that can be found far below the surface.”

“When I was young, I’d attach a rope to my waist and tie it to a spike I’d drive into the ice. I loved climbing down into those gaps. It was both amazing and terrifying.”

“What did your parents think about you doing that?”

“Honestly? I didn’t tell them. But like the ocean is in your blood, the ice calls to me. It’s part of my soul.”

"I can't imagine. We get snow here in the winter, but it melts fast, and we have no glaciers. The only ice I've dealt with is some coating my windshield after a storm or slippery roads when I drive to work and walk inside my shop. Most businesses in town remain open all year round, though I don't imagine my ice cream shop will make much during the winter. No one seems to want to eat ice cream when it's freezing outside."

"I would." He squeezed my hand. "You know it's pretty much a cliché that you own an ice cream shop, and I'm an ice lord."

"I thought of that. I can handle the jokes that might circulate around town. Can you?"

"Absolutely."

"I used to drop my things about here." I pointed farther up the shore. Kraken's Keep, an exclusive seafood restaurant, was open, and people sat on the deck enjoying their meals and the view of the sea. "I would bring an umbrella and a folding chair, tying everything onto a red wagon Grannie kept in the garage."

"That must've been hard to pull across the sand," he said.

"I was a determined kid. I wanted to be at the beach, and I wanted to enjoy it in comfort. I bet if I ever go camping, I'd bring a big mixer and an extension cord I could plug in to run it."

Pausing, he frowned down at me. I liked how the moonlight played on his features, lighting his blue skin to an iciness I found incredibly sexy. "Why?"

"So I could make pizza dough."

"With the mixer."

"I mean, I can make it without one, I suppose, but it's nice to have a dough hook to do the hard work for you."

"How would you cook your pizza?" He still didn't look convinced. Truly, he needed to go camping with me, something I'd only done a few times when Grannie sent me to summer programs as a teenager.

"On the grill, of course. You stretch it out and carefully lay it on the oiled grate. When it's partly done and browning nicely on the bottom, you flip it over and top it with cheese and everything else. You cover the grill and let it smoke and bake. Complete yum."

"I've got to try that sometime."

"Have you ever been camping?"

"A few times, if you count sleeping in an ice cabin."

"Brr." I hugged my waist. "You lay on ice?"

"My family owns an exclusive business. People and monsters come from all over the world to sleep inside our ice cabins and watch the northern lights ripple across the sky. Because they want to retire, my brother plans to take over the business from my parents soon. We don't lay on the ice. Each cabin has a full array of fake fur bedding, plus squishy furniture you can snuggle up on. Imagine sipping cocoa as you sit outside covered with blankets, staring up at the stars while the northern lights sway across the sky in blues, pinks, and greens."

"It sounds amazing." And fun.

"I'll go camping with you sometime—and we can make pizza—if you'll travel with me a different time to stay in an ice cabin."

"It's a deal."

We continued walking, sharing our favorite pizza

toppings and the food we might eat when we stayed in one of his family's ice cabins. I liked that he could picture me there with him, that he wanted to share something special like that with me.

"You must've gotten sunburned during those summers spent here on the beach," he said.

"Not too much. I—well, Grannie—was careful. Even though I promised to stay out of the sun and put on sunscreen, she always insisted I wear a long-sleeved shirt that blocked UV rays, plus a big hat. I'm glad she made me do it, though I grumbled a lot back then. I still love the feel of the sun on my skin. It's part of the ocean. They kiss a lot and are very happy together."

"*They* kiss, huh?" Stopping, he turned to face me. "Who exactly are you talking about?"

"The sun and the ocean. The sunlight swoops down and kisses the crests of the sea, making it sparkle with pleasure. Haven't you seen that?"

"Right now, the ocean is cheating on the sun with the moon. I see lots of sparkling going on offshore."

"It's a reverse harem," I quipped. "The ocean has *two* lovers, not just one."

"Two, huh? What about you, Melly? Would you want two lovers?"

"I guess it depends on what the first lover has to offer and what he doesn't." My face ached from my grin. I started walking again. "Maybe a second could deliver what the first can't handle all on his own."

Elrik huffed and swooped after me, splashing through the water to pick me up into his arms. Turning, he strode deeper into the water as it surged around his thighs. He held me in his outstretched arms, growling as he threatened to dip me into the waves.

I squealed and clung to his shoulders, wrapping my legs around his chest. My sundress dipped into the water, but so far, my body hadn't. "Stop, stop!"

"Maybe you need to sample what your first lover can offer before you start dreaming about a second," he said with a smirk. "You don't know what you're missing."

"My first lover hasn't yet made an offer."

He stilled, staring down at me with a hint of vulnerability in his glacier eyes. "And if he did?"

"I believe he'd have to try it to find out what I might say," I said softly. Heat coasted through my veins. I couldn't wait to see where this might go next.

"Your *potential* lover has been waiting for you to say she's ready," he said gruffly, his sapphire gaze locked on mine.

"Perhaps I've also been waiting since my *potential* lover made a vow not to get involved with anyone."

"A vow that he has thrown away."

"Completely?"

He grinned. "Completely."

"Then I'm ready."

"Just like that?" he said, his eyes widening.

"Just like that."

"Mate," he growled against my throat. "You smell wonderful, like the sea and chocolate, and just you."

This felt right. So right.

"Mate," I said with all the emotions buried deep within my heart. "If you stay at my place tonight, we'll have to be careful."

"My home isn't an option. We need to stay close to your grandmother in case she needs us."

I loved that he cared enough for her to feel that way.

He frowned, clearly thinking. "I could drive away and park my truck in the supermarket lot a few blocks over. I could walk back if this means you're inviting me into your apartment."

"I am." I winked at him. "Let's go back to my apartment, where we can talk about what my potential first lover might have to offer."

"I don't want to talk." He pivoted and strode from the water and up the shore. "I want to show."

16

ELRIK

"You're like a spring thaw to my endless winter, both gentle and relentless," I said as I carried her along the beach and toward the bench where we'd left our shoes.

"That's so sweet, Elrik," she sighed against my skin.

"Your warmth softens the ice surrounding my heart, carving out a sanctuary where none existed before." Now that the damn had let loose, the words poured from me. "My ice-bound soul trembles at the thought of showing you how much you're coming to mean to me."

I only paused to scoop up our shoes, handing them to her one by one.

"I can walk," she said with a laugh.

"Do you want to?" The last thing I wanted to do was make her feel embarrassed. I sensed she was as worried about her reputation as her grandmother.

"I like being in your arms, Elrik." Her eyes scanned the area. "We're alone. And I find I actually don't care what anyone else thinks."

"I like holding you in my arms."

"I can't say that anyone has ever swooped me up like this before, let alone carried me more than a foot or so."

"Or threatened to dip you into the sea?"

"I wouldn't have minded that. She's warm right now. Comforting. We should come here at night and go swimming, though we'll have to watch out for sharks."

"Sharks won't come near a monster."

"It's funny. I don't see you as a monster. The term has changed since orcs and centaurs started moving close to us. Monster was a term used to scare children. Today's kids will grow up thinking monsters are nice people."

"You don't know how much it means to all of us that we're accepted." Mostly, that is. There were always a few who sneered when they saw us, and there had even been a few protests in front of our embassy, but in general, we were welcomed into human society.

"I know many were frightened at first. All those stories about the boogeyman haunting our dreams."

I carried her down the street. We passed a couple, and the male yeti nodded. The male human grinned and wiggled his eyebrows. While many married within their own species like they had before, other monsters had found mates among the humans. It was becoming more and more common to see couples of all sorts of species together.

"Boogeymen are under your bed too," I point out.

Her eyes widened and her lips quivered, though with humor. "You're kidding me, right?"

I grin. "Am I?"

"Fuck."

"Not often."

"Fuck!"

A centaur trotting by on the street huffed. "Please. Kids might be around."

"Hey, sorry." She cringed. "Potty mouth here."

"I can't believe you didn't know the boogeyman is real," I said.

Her face scrunched in a cute way. "Really real?"

"Really."

"Hmm."

At the end of her driveway, I placed her on her feet and stroked her cheek. "Do you want to wait inside?"

"The night's gorgeous. Warm and sultry. I'll stay here."

Talk about incentive to make me hurry. I started up my truck and backed out onto the road, driving to the lot and parking.

In no time, I stood in front of Melly again.

I lifted her into my arms and aimed for the exterior staircase leading to her apartment above the garage.

"About the boogeyman," she said.

"Hmm?"

"I mean, some people might find the thought of a monster beneath their bed sexy. Does he have tentacles?"

I came to a complete stop at the bottom of the stairs. "What?"

"Tentacles. You know, those long limbs with suction cups all over them."

"I know what you mean," I growled.

She frowned, tilting her head as she looked up at me.

"You sound irritated. Are you jealous of what the tentacled boogeyman might do to my body?"

I huffed. "You haven't yet discovered what an ice lord can do to your body, so no."

She crooked her neck to look up the stairs. "Why are you stopping?"

"Let's get one thing straight. No boogeyman, tentacled or not, is putting one finger—or limb—on your body."

Her laugh spurted out, though she kept her voice low. "If you don't mind, I'll try out an ice lord before I decide something like that."

I bolted, taking the stairs two at a time and only paused for her to enter the code on her door to unlock it. Inside, I kicked the door shut, secured it, and snarled. "Bedroom?"

She waved her hand. "My boogeyman abode is through the kitchen and the first door on the left. There's only one bedroom in the apartment, actually. I imagine you—and the boogeyman with luscious tentacles—can find it."

She was such a tease. I was going to make her pay for every word said to prick my heart.

I raced across her kitchen and into her bedroom, where I tossed her onto the monster-sized bed and crawled on top of her.

17

MELLY

There was nothing better than an out of control ice lord.

My ice lord, that is.

He tossed me onto the bed and joined me, his forearms caging my arms, his mouth claiming mine.

I clung to him, on fire for him already. Funny how it hadn't taken me long to realize I wanted to be with this guy in every way possible. Need pounded through me, and the only thing grounding me was my hands on his shoulders.

His tongue stroked its way past my lips, the only barrier to my mouth and probably my heart. Our mouths moved together and like he was the fire to dry wood, I caught flame. I feverishly tugged at his shirt, wanting it off, craving the feel of his skin on mine.

He lifted his head. "You're sure?"

"About everything," I breathed. "Clothing. Off. Show me what you can offer." The last came out in a teasing tone.

"Yes, ma'am," he said with a grin. He wrenched his shirt up over his head and tossed it aside.

I took in the play of muscles across his smooth blue chest, the way his abs rippled as he held himself above me. With a fingertip, I traced his pecs and meandered down his sternum to the rows of taut muscles flexing across his belly. "You must work out all the time."

"Ice climbing. Hiking. Repairing ice cabins. Rock climbing. Search and rescue where we go for days without stopping, determined to find whoever is lost."

"That's amazing. I imagine it's scary but wonderful when you locate them."

"It gave me a purpose when I needed one most."

I sensed there was more to his family story than just an older brother who was distant, one who apparently had no qualms about stealing his younger brother's girlfriend. Slime, that's what he was, and I'd shout it in his face if I ever met him. I'd want to shout it, that is. I wouldn't do anything to embarrass Elrik or myself.

But I didn't want to think about that right now. I wanted to show him that I adored everything about him, that I wanted him above all others.

His mouth fell on mine again, hot and demanding, and I gave way, any barrier I might've erected around my heart falling to let in this male alone.

He tugged my sundress up, bunching it in his big fist, until there was nothing between us but my skimpy panties and bra.

Leaving my mouth, he kissed along my jaw and down my neck, nibbling as he went. My skin caught flame wherever he touched, and as he teased his tongue across my overheated skin, my moan ripped out.

He stroked my thigh, his hand creating swirling patterns that crept closer and closer to my core. I was feverish already, thrusting my hips up. I craved his hand there. His fingers. His mouth. His cock.

He eased my underwear down, and I kicked it away. My bra soon followed. And when he nudged my thighs apart, I spread them eagerly.

He lifted his head and watched my face as he traced his finger through my wetness. His groan ripped out. "You're amazing. I want you very much." He kept his eyes locked on mine as he dipped a finger inside me. "Fuck. So wet for me. So tight. I can't wait to sink my cock into your pretty pussy, to feel it clench around me as you come, to hear your cry as you give in to your pleasure."

He thrust a finger deep, and my guttural moan echoed in the room. And when his thumb found my clit and stroked it, I gasped and jerked my hips up to meet his hand.

I wanted his mouth down there and on my breasts. My belly. Everywhere he wanted to lick and suck.

He kissed me again while his hand performed magic between my legs. Finally, his head lifted, and he gave me the sweetest smile. "I'm going to taste you. Come for me while I do it, would you?"

I had a feeling I'd be coming more than once tonight. I nodded and tipped my head back, smiling as he sucked on one nipple, then the other. They formed tight beads, and when he gently nibbled, I couldn't hold back my cry of pleasure.

He kissed across my belly and crawled between my legs, pulling his fingers out of my body only to replace them with his mouth. His very long, thick tongue stroked my inner walls so nicely. His fingers rolled my clit.

This man knew how to ply a woman's body, and I was so lost in what he was doing, I didn't have time to wonder where he'd learned this skill.

He lifted his head, his finger replacing his tongue, stroking my inner walls and driving my body ever higher. "There's only me for you and you for me. No one is ever going to come between us."

"I want you, Elrik. You. No one else."

He plunged his fingers deep within me, curling them, pulling them out only to drive them inside me again. His thumb remained on my clit, rubbing in a way that drove me into a frenzy. "When I'm with you, all I want to do is kiss you. I need to keep my hands on you because when we're not touching, I feel lost. From the moment I met you at that wedding, you were the only one I could see, the only one I wanted to be with like this. You're perfect. Precious. And I'm going to show you how wonderful you are every single day of your life."

"Elrik," I groaned.

He eased up and kissed me, and I tasted myself on his tongue. I'd never thought something that simple could be arousing, but that combined with his fingers moving inside me sent me to the edge and thrust me over the other side.

An orgasm crashed through me, and I rode it, holding on tight while his fingers moved within me and his tongue stroked mine.

18

ELRIK

Melly was responsive. Precious. Infinitely desirable.

And she was all mine.

I rode her orgasm, milking it out with my fingers until she collapsed beneath me.

Lifting my head, I watched the pleasure continue to unfold on her face.

"Elrik," she groaned. "What are you doing to me?"

"Showing you how much you mean to me."

"I want you. All of you."

It was time to claim her completely.

Rising from the bed, I stripped off my jeans. My cock ached with need, and it sprung up to smack against my abs.

She stared at it, and I watched her face to see if she cringed or if her excitement remained. I found only eagerness there, but . . .

"I'm big. Sorry." Why did I feel like wincing about something beyond my control?

The smile she sent me made my insides flip in all directions. "I think big is going to be a wonderful thing. You'll fit."

"You're sure?"

She scooted to the edge of the bed and got onto her knees, facing me. "Give me your cock. I want to play with it a bit." Her fingertips teased across my hip, moving closer to my shaft that throbbed so much, I worried it would explode.

My groan ripped out. "If you touch it, I'm going to come."

"Then come. We'll give you a short time to rest, and when you're ready again, we'll keep going."

"It's not fair to you."

"I just had a wonderful orgasm. If that's all I get tonight, I'm okay with that. Expect me to be demanding and needy in the morning, however."

My laugh snorted out. This was why this woman was my mate; she could see humor in a situation that was too often serious. She was relaxed about this, not pressuring me or herself for more than what came naturally.

And she'd come so wonderfully from my fingers.

She slid her fingers across my abdomen to my cock and took it in both hands. "Yummy."

"It's not food."

"Oh, yes, it is." When she looked up at me, I read so much mischief on her face, my balls tightened, and my cock spasmed. I wasn't coming—not yet—but damn, I was close. I'd think of ice to distract me. How tired I sometimes was after climbing deep into a crevasse and making my way back to the surface.

Of lint. Dryer lint to be exact.

As she leaned close and breathed on the head of my cock, I tried to remember when I'd last cleaned out my dryer's lint trap. Two weeks? Surely neglecting it that long was a fire hazard. I needed to remember to take care of it the moment I got home.

She sucked the head of my cock into her mouth. My balls spasmed, and my cock bobbed upward, seeking her warmth, her wetness.

My groan echoed in the room. Tipping my head back, I closed my eyes, and gave myself over to this wonderful woman who was eager to please me.

My balls tightened, and my body started to shudder.

I erected a barrier between my mind and my shaft.

Did anyone ever collect enough dryer lint to have it spun into yarn? It would make nice mittens or . . . a scarf for a toy poodle.

Her mouth was hot and her tongue lightly scratchy. She dragged it up and down my length and it was all I could do to focus on lint.

Then she pointed my cock her way and took a big gulp of me, sucking so much of me inside her hot mouth, I worried I'd choke off her airway. Her wide eyes met mine as she moved her mouth and sucked, and damn, but there wasn't anything prettier than my mate taking as much of me as she could.

I slid my fingers into her hair, taking care not to tug, and pumped slowly toward me. When she hummed, the vibration ricocheted down my cock. I nearly shot myself inside her.

Her fingertips stroked my balls, and they liked that as

much as my cock did her mouth. Her tongue. Her humming that was making my brain shoot out the top of my head and through the roof.

Pulling back, she released me with a wet pop. "I'm going to suck you off soon, but I want to feel this big boy buried inside me." She turned and rose onto her hands and knees, pointing her gorgeous, ripe ass my way. She was dripping so much I worried it would run down the back of her thigh, and I'd miss out on it. "Ride me, cowboy," she said over her shoulder. "Come on. You know you want to do it."

"I was thinking of dryer lint and poodles and scarves."

The prettiest smile rose on her face. "Whatever gets you off. Come on. Stick that big old cock inside me. Drive it in hard, would you?"

"Not at first," I protested, my heart flailing like a ninety-year-old maiden.

"Later, then? Because I need it. Want it. Want you."

"Alright. You've talked me into it," I huffed.

Stooping forward, I licked her opening, groaning at how amazing she tasted. Just a few more samples . . . I drove my tongue inside her. When she whimpered and pressed back to meet me, I found her clit and rubbed it hard while sliding my tongue across her inner walls, coating her with my saliva while savoring her natural wetness.

When she started gasping and rocking hard against my mouth and my fingers, I rose up over her and placed the head of my cock at her opening.

Then I held her hips and drove myself deep inside her.

19

MELLY

"Tell me if it hurts, if I'm too much," he growled behind me.

My mind was already spinning with pleasure. I'd almost come just from his first thrust. He was big, yes, but he felt amazing. "More."

I gripped the blankets and he started to move, pulling all the way out before pushing in hard again. My eyes pretty much rolled back in my head, and my moans kept bursting out with each of his slow, heady thrusts.

"Too much?" he snarled.

I peeked over my shoulder, finding his muscles tight, his face taut with pleasure. He wanted to let go. I could tell. But he was taking this as carefully as he could to keep from hurting me.

If I wasn't half in love with him already, this would push me over the edge.

Most guys would've given into their own desire already. What I might get out of it would come second if my needs occurred to them at all.

"You can go faster, push harder," I snarled into the blankets.

He snorted. Laughing? I hoped not crying. "I'm going fast enough."

"Actually, you're not. Faster!"

His pace slowed to a delicious thrust that buried him deep within me before he snapped his hips back to pull his cock out. "What if it hurts you?"

"I'll tell you. I bet it won't."

"I bet it will."

I peered back at him. "What do you want to bet?"

"Like . . . money?"

"Well, no. I can't imagine that would be fun. Something creative. If it hurts, I'll tell you, and you'll slow and try not to plunge too deep. And you'll win, I guess. For your prize, I'll suck you off later."

"You said you were going to do that already."

"Then maybe you've already won."

"That's not how this works."

"My pussy. My prize."

He scowled. "And if it doesn't hurt?" His face was tight, and a bead of sweat coiled down the side of his face. I wanted to lick it. Lick his neck and make him bunch his muscles like he was doing right now so I could glide my tongue across those as well.

"If it hurts, we'll still both have lots of fun, and as my prize, I get to suck you off in the morning."

He barked out a laugh. "Seems like I win no matter what."

"Which is why you need to go faster!"

"Alright. I'm going to do it. I'm not going to think

about lint and poodle scarves any longer."

I had to explore this later. "That's a relief."

"It really is. It's hard."

"I like it hard."

He snorted. "No, really?"

"Show me I'm yours," I said. "Prove it with your cock and your body. I'll let you know if it causes any pain." I had a feeling it was going to be amazing. I couldn't believe I had to talk him into doing this. Again, he was the opposite of most guys. But Elrik was nothing like any other male I'd met.

I was going to keep him if I could, starting tonight.

"I want you to roar when you come," I said. "Will you do that for me?"

"I can try." He was still holding back, pulling out and pushing back into me hard enough to make my toes curl but not fiercely enough to make me go wild beneath him.

"Show me."

"You're mine."

"I am. Prove it. Claim me as your mate, because I'm going to be doing the same as I take you into my body."

"Mine," he growled, starting to move faster, pushing inside me harder.

"That's the spirit." My grin split my face, and it was a wonder I could focus now that he was giving me everything I needed. "More, Elrik. Earn that reward."

He went feral, leaning over me, touching me everywhere. While his cock plunged inside me and pulled back out, his hand reached for my breasts, rolling one nipple after the other. Each tug sent shockwaves to my core. His other hand stroked my clit, and it was all I could do to hold back. I wanted to come so bad, but I wanted to do it while this male roared.

I was a whimpering wreck, pushing back to meet his body, spreading my thighs wider. Pressure built inside me, winding tighter and tighter. Cries erupted from deep within me with each of his thrusts.

When I thought it couldn't get any better, he gripped my hips with one hand, his other still locked on my clit. He went completely wild, bucking against me. It was all I could do to remain in place. But oh, how wonderful it was. A fusion of me and him and our hearts and our minds.

Pure bliss.

With each of his thrusts, I soared higher. I could feel his cock getting stiffer. He was close, but so was I.

"Now, Elrik," I panted.

"Ready?"

"Now!"

"Take all of me, mate," he shouted, his hips a blur, and his cock a rigid pole driving deep inside me.

I couldn't hold off much longer, but I wanted to feel it all. His cock spasming deep within me, his cry of joy, the shudders of his body.

"You're mine," he growled in my ear.

"Yours."

His fingers and his cock drove me over the edge, and I stiffened, my body giving way to a gush of pleasure.

His cock started jerking inside me, and he rode me through the best orgasm of my life.

And he roared.

20

ELRIK

She was perfect. Beautiful. Precious.

And my mate.

With my cock still buried deep inside her, I eased us to the side, taking her with me, spooning her with my body.

"You're mine," I growled again. I kept saying it over and over.

"Yours," she kept replying.

We drifted to sleep, and I didn't wake until dawn was cracking open the day and light started peeking in through the window.

I sensed her waking as well. She reached back and stroked my hip, her fingers moving inward until she could wrap them around my cock. I'd been inside her twice during the night, first with her riding me and the second time when she sucked me off as she'd promised.

We'd both won, and I couldn't be a happier ice lord.

My phone buzzed. I should ignore it. But it could be a message from my family. My parents weren't young any longer, and Dad kept insisting he was perfectly safe hiking across glaciers alone. I disagreed.

I rolled onto my back and grabbed my phone off the bedside table, scrolling into it.

"Oh," I said.

Melly rose up onto her elbow. "Oh?"

"It's Katar. Sue wasn't feeling well, and she went to the doctor. She called him to let him know in case we still had questions. She's worried they'll admit her to the hospital again."

"Oh, my gosh." Melly slid from the bed and tugged on a robe. "Do you think she'll be okay?"

"We'll find out."

"I'll text her. I want to go see her. I'll stop by Fairytale Florals before work and buy her some flowers. Carla can cover the shop until I get back. Assuming anyone plans to stop by for ice cream at a place with such a horrible rating."

"Not everyone reads online reviews."

"I'll try some of the strategies I used initially to draw in customers. Free samples. Coupons. Advertising. I haven't had to do any of that since the first week I opened, but I need good reviews to balance the rest. I hope the PR person has come up with other ideas."

"I hope so too." I got up. "Breakfast before you leave?"

"I'd love to, but I need to check on Grannie and set things out for her before I leave."

I rounded the bed and tugged her into my arms, holding her for one moment. Life was thrusting itself between us, and it would be some time before we could step back into just us once more.

“Do you want to have dinner tonight?” she asked. “I could cook again.”

“Why don’t I get takeout for the three of us from Kraken’s Keep?”

“That sounds wonderful. Four-thirty? Grannie prefers to eat early. She likes to be sitting in the living room with her feet up and her knitting on her lap before it gets dark.”

“Perfect. Any preferences as far as food goes?”

“We like just about anything.”

She stepped backward and grabbed some clothing from her bureau. “What’s on your agenda today?”

“I’m going to question Bob.”

“Fill me in later?”

“Sure. After dinner, we could take another walk on the beach.”

“I’d love that.”

“Last night was special.” I watched her face and was rewarded when she sent me a sultry smile.

“Very special. Um . . .” Her gaze fell. “You could stay again tonight if you want.”

“Oh, yes, I want.” I strode over to her and swept her pretty hair across her shoulder. “I’ll park at the supermarket again and walk over after dark.”

She hugged me quickly before backing away. “No talking about lint tonight.”

“You mean you don’t want me collecting lint and turning it into a dog scarf?”

Her laugh snorted out, which was my intention. “You’re silly sometimes. I like it.”

Then I’d keep dreaming up ways to make her laugh.

She went to take a shower. Whistling between my teeth, I left her apartment and walked to my truck, driving to Bob's home. I'd called the day before, and he said I could come by early, that he woke at five every morning and by eight he would've had his breakfast and his mind would be sharpest.

I knocked on the door and a woman about thirty-five years old opened it. "Elrik?"

I showed her my ID and she let me inside, urging me to follow her into the living room to the right of the entrance. "Bob's in here." Her gaze sought mine, and she frowned. "I'm not sure what this is about. I'm Ginny, his caregiver, by the way."

She was Rose's younger sister's stepdaughter. Ex-step-daughter since they'd divorced.

"I'm investigating the poisoning on behalf of Grannie Rose," I said.

"I see. She didn't do it."

"I don't think so either."

"I don't know who did, but it couldn't be her. She's too sweet. Too kind."

Inside the living room, I settled on the sofa. Bob sat on a recliner with his feet up. His gaze took in my tall frame, narrowing as he studied my eyes. I wasn't sure what conclusion he drew, but his face relaxed.

A large metal device with a canvas sling had been collapsed and parked near the wall, and I had no idea what it was.

"That's Bob's lift," Ginny said. "He's not able to get around on his own any longer, and with his macular degeneration, he can't see well either. I use the lift to get him out of his bed and into his chair."

"If I could, I'd stand to greet you," Bob said in a crotchety voice.

"No problem."

"What can I do for you today, Elrik?" His gaze drifted across Ginny before settling on me again.

I didn't know much about macular degeneration other than it was a degenerative disease of the eyes and that the person usually lost their sight. Once it had progressed, they weren't completely blind, but they couldn't see well enough to drive or do many daily tasks.

"I wanted to question you about the night of the poisoning," I said.

"Of course. Have a seat," Bob said.

I dropped into a chair near the coffee table. "Could you tell me when you arrived that night?"

"I was the last one inside, like usual," Bob said. "Ginny brings me in the handicap van I bought. It has an amazing lift like the one we use here."

"You can't walk at all?"

He shook his head. "Haven't been able to do that for years. I use an electric scooter to get around most of the time. It's amazing mobility."

I had a hard time believing that someone who couldn't see well and wasn't ambulatory could've poisoned the punch, but I had to question everyone who was there that evening.

"Ginny brings me to the social club event each week," he said. "Which is quite kind of her. She gets me out of the van and brings me inside."

"I usually sit in the van while the social club members meet," Ginny said. "I scroll on my phone. Read. I've got three thousand followers on TickingClock, so I make some videos for that and post them. Gotta keep my followers happy."

"I stay in my chair throughout the evening, and the others are nice enough to help me with my food and drinks," Bob said.

"Did you have any punch that night?" I asked.

"Never have. Never will." His lips tightened. "It's much too sweet for my taste. Contrary to popular belief, not *everyone* loves Rose's punch."

"I don't think it's that bad," Ginny said. Her gaze met mine. "Grannie Rose used to make it around the holidays, and everyone loved it."

"What did you do after you arrived?" I asked Bob.

"Let me see." Frowning, he tapped his temple. "My mind's not quite what it used to be, sadly. Part of my disease process. If I remember correctly, I was sitting there like usual, waiting for someone to bring me a plate of food. Not shoving myself to the head of the line like all the others usually do. As Ginny said, everyone thinks Rose's punch is amazing. They're like wild dogs sniffing prey. All over it whenever she serves it."

"Even when Melly makes it for her," Ginny said. "Which she did while Rose was in rehab and even after she got home. It was only that last night that Rose made it herself like she used to. Sometimes, Melly drops her grandmother off like I do Bob. But while I wait in the parking lot, Melly drives away." She huffed. "Maybe next time, she'll stay around in case Grannie needs her."

"Come now," Bob said. "You know Rose is doing fine. She might've needed help when she first came home from rehab, but she's weaning herself off that walker quite quickly." He smiled in a reminiscent way. "She's still quite the woman. Rose was something else in her day. I asked her out a few times. Did you know that? She shot me down each and every time."

"I imagine she liked you well enough," Ginny said with a shrug. "Just not enough to date you."

"Her loss." Bob grinned. "All that's water under the bridge now."

I'd pretty much ruled Bob out. He wasn't mobile, he could barely see, and these things weren't something anyone could fake. Grannie Rose turning him down a few times years ago wasn't a strong enough motive to frame someone for poisoning others. It appeared he'd had no way to reach the punch on his own. He arrived last, after the punch had been made. As for Ginny, she'd brought Bob inside and it sounded like he kept her busy until she went to the parking lot to wait. "You said people started getting sick shortly after you arrived?"

He frowned again. "I think so." His face cleared. "Oh, yes, I remember now. Alfred vomited, then Sue. Not sure if hers was sympathy vomiting or not. You know how it is. Someone vomits and before you know it, the smell hits you hard in the sinuses, and it's all you can do to hold down your cookies."

"How did you know it was Sue and Alfred?" He couldn't see well.

"Their voices." He tapped his earlobe. "I don't see well, and my memory can be faulty, but my hearing's as sharp as ever. I could kind of see them out of the periphery of my vision. They were bent over the big black trash bucket the janitor leaves for us. Hazel and Carla weren't far behind in vomiting." He tsked. "It was a damn shame actually. Other than samples the police took of the dishes, everything got thrown out. We get to take food home after the evening, and I look forward to it. I bring bread as my contribution. Store-bought cookies. It's not much, but it's an offering for the potluck. Ginny picks them up for me in advance. As my reward, I come home with at least three home cooked meals from the leftovers."

Ginny's concerned gaze swept across Bob. "I'll keep taking him to the socials for as long as I can."

"If they ever start back up again, that is." Bob's lips thinned. "I probably shouldn't bother going any longer. It's not like I can dance, though I sway in my chair. But I like to get out, and I don't know how much longer I'll get to do it. I look forward to it each week even though I can't play poker any longer. Can't see the cards or follow the play; not like I used to. But I eat with everyone else and visit."

Ginny stared toward the ceiling, clearly thinking. "Grannie was in the bathroom when Bob arrived. Sue and Alfred were near the punchbowl with Hazel and Carla. Everyone held cups of punch, and I remember Alfred joking that he'd had three cups already. Sue laughed and said she'd had four. The bowl was almost empty."

"That's the way it always is," Bob said. "That punch goes fast. In addition to cookies and bread, I usually bring a few bottles of ginger ale, which I drink instead of the punch. I have to drink diet. Once the punch is gone, the rest drink ginger ale while they play poker. I sit nearby and listen. That's almost as much fun."

"I asked Alfred and Sue if they had something contagious, because I would've whipped Bob around and taken him back to the van," Ginny said firmly. "He can't afford to get sick. Even a cold could wipe him out for a week or more."

"Compromised immune system," Bob offered. "Sometimes, living sucks. Don't you agree?" His cackle rang out. "But it sure beats the alternative."

"I'm sorry," I said.

Bob grunted. "Don't get old, son. Don't get old."

Kind of hard not to, but I knew what he meant. I stood. "I think that's all the questions I have, but if I think of anything else, I'll call."

Ginny rose. "I'll write down my number. Call me, and I'll ask Bob and get back to you."

"Thank you."

She walked me to the door. "It was nice meeting you."

"You as well." I had a few things to think about. Clues that might lead to nothing and others that might tie this all together. I still had no idea who might have spiked the punch, however.

"If you see Rose, tell her I'll drop off the paperwork next week," Ginny said as she opened the front door.

"Paperwork?"

"In addition to caring for Bob, I pretty much run his business." Pride shone in her voice.

"What paperwork are you talking about?"

“Everyone knows, so I’m not sharing confidential information. Grannie fell and broke her hip at the church function room a few months back. Bob’s business held the liability policy for the church. But Grannie said she’s not going to sue for damages despite her slipping on a big glob of floor polish. The janitor must’ve missed it when she was cleaning prior to the social.” Ginny leaned close and lowered her voice. “Bob doesn’t know that I’ve worked with Grannie, that I made sure the extra cost of her rehab was covered by the insurance company in exchange for her signing off on anything further.”

More twists in the plot? “What’s the name of Bob’s insurance company?”

“Everyone knows that too. Sterling. Sterling Life and Indemnity.”

21

MELLY

I texted Sue, and she said she was not going to be admitted to the hospital. When I told her I wanted to stop by, she asked me to wait a day or two, saying she was much too tired for guests.

Worry kept stabbing through me. Was she getting sicker? Her loss would rip me to pieces, but there didn't seem to be much I could do about it.

When I reached the ice cream shop, I discovered Carla's PR firm had come through. They'd reached out to the Mystic Harbor website admin and gotten all the one-star ratings removed. They couldn't take down the reviews, because they could be legitimate, but they agreed that a flash of one-star ratings all at once had come from a troll. This brought Creature Cone's average up to a little over four, which was much better than where it was yesterday.

The PR firm also posted on the town's FaceSpace page and Instaplug, talking up my business with some amazing graphics, and they were not only getting lots of likes, but the comments were also very encouraging. They had a few other strategies they planned to deploy over the next week, such as videos on TickingClock, and I felt like I could relax for a bit. It was lovely having someone who knew what they were doing handling this.

People started to trickle into my shop mid-afternoon. Yay.

Elrik strolled in and sat at a table while we took care of our customers.

"Go hang out with him if you want," Carla said, tilting her head his way. "I can cover this."

"Are you sure?"

She nodded and took the next customer's order while I walked over to stand beside his table.

He stood. "I set up an appointment to speak with Hazel. If you can come with me, great. If not, I'll let you know what I discover, if anything."

"Go," Carla called out with a laugh.

"You're sure?" I asked.

"Go!"

"Alright. Hazel's studio, Boogey Beasts, is right next door." I waved to the brick wall dividing us. "At one point, Hazel wanted to expand her studio into this space as well, but Grannie told her no."

"More pole dancing?" he asked.

"She planned on offering yoga classes here, but Grannie had already promised me this space for my ice cream shop. The location's perfect on Main Street."

Carla grunted, and after the customers left, she walked over to join us.

"You're right. The location's perfect for any business,"

she said. “There isn’t much property available anywhere in town, let alone on Main Street.”

“Were you able to secure the location you wanted in Seashell Cove?” I asked, then explained to Elrik. “Carla’s an amazing artist. Her paintings of the coast are stunning.”

A blush filled Carla’s face. “Thank you, Melly. I appreciate you saying that.”

“At one point, she thought about renting this space to display her art and run shows.”

“That was when I had big dreams of selling my seascapes,” Carla said. “But, no, I didn’t rent the location in Seashell Cove. I’ve . . . put that on hold for now.”

Cashflow could be the reason why she wasn’t setting up a storefront yet.

“My offer for you to put some of your artwork up for sale here still stands.” I waved to the blank walls. “You can showcase your work, and as it sells, replace it with more. Anytime. I mean it.”

“Thank you, but that’s a dream I should give up.”

I hated to see her sad, but she had a lot to deal with right now. Maybe selling her artwork could be done at a different time. “Your dream is worth pursuing,” I still pointed out.

“I said no,” she snapped, a scowl transforming her face. “I’m not going to put my art up here.” Her scowl disappeared as fast as it rose.

While I thought her art would sell here, I had no reason to force her into placing it on our walls. “Alright.”

Elrik frowned, looking between us, but said nothing.

More customers came in, and Carla stomped over to serve them.

Elrik and I left Creature Cones. Once the door had shut behind us, he stopped me on the sidewalk and drew me over close to the big plate glass window with ice cream cones and other delectable treats painted on the glossy surface.

"Tell me more about Carla's art," Elki said softly.

"She's painted all her life, and it's gorgeous. Like, New York show quality beautiful. She talked to Grannie about renting the space, but I'd already spoken to my grandmother about my dream of opening an ice cream shop, so Grannie told her no."

He frowned.

I tilted my head. "You're looking for a motive in her art?"

"Let's step back a bit. What would Carla gain by pinning the poisoning on Grannie?"

"I can't think of anything other than Walter dating Grannie before Carla. She was mad enough about him considering divorce to make threats. And I'm sure she was pissed off when she discovered he'd sold most of the shares in his company. When I lay it out like that, she has plenty of motive. Anger will make people do things they'd never otherwise consider. But Walter's dead. It's been a long time since all this happened. Why wait until now to act?"

"It has been a long time."

"I guess I can't see her doing something like this."

"She wanted your space."

"So did Hazel. But I'm not sure if wanting this spot on

Main Street is a solid enough motive for someone to do such a horrible thing to my grandmother."

He shrugged. "As you said, people do weird things when they're angry. Ginny said everyone believed you'd be making the punch that night."

"Because I'd done it for a while. It wasn't long after Grannie got home from rehab that she started going to the socials and supervising me making the punch." My low laugh rang out. "She couldn't stand long, so she'd sit nearby and direct me." I frowned, thinking. "We need to consider the idea that someone was trying to frame me, not my grandmother." This opened all sorts of new avenues.

Rapid footsteps came our way, and we turned, watching as the nurse who had been caring for Sue at the hospital hurried in our direction.

She stopped beside us and peered around before leaning close and lowering her voice to a bare whisper. "I'm Pauline, but you can't remember my name."

"I'm Melly, and this is Elrik. Why shouldn't we remember your name?"

Elrik shot me a raised-eyebrow look, but I was as puzzled as him.

"I could get into trouble for this, so I didn't see you. I didn't speak with you. You didn't see or speak with me either. Confidentiality and all that."

"I see." Though I truly didn't.

"About your friend, Sue," Pauline said.

My shoulders drooped. "I've known her all my life. She and my grandmother have been best friends since they were in school together."

"I could tell that you care for her."

I sniffed. "Very much. I'm sad about her prognosis, about what this means for her."

"Yeah, that's just it." Pauline winced through a swallow. "Her kidneys didn't take a hit, though *I* didn't tell you that."

I blinked slowly. "I don't know what you mean. She was just at her doctor's this morning."

"Was she?" Her eyebrows lifted.

"Why would she lie about something like this?" Elrik asked.

"No idea," Pauline said. "But you might want to ask her. See, when she came into the hospital after drinking the Xylitol-spiked punch, they were worried her kidneys might suffer. Xylitol's mostly excreted by the liver, but it's also hard on the kidneys, so who knows what a big dose of the artificial sweetener might've done if she hadn't come in right away. But she did. We gave her fluids and dextrose, of course, and kept her a few nights for observation. The ER probably would've just run some labs, then discharged her, and they told her that. But after her boyfriend was seen by the doctor, he hurried to her side, and she announced that kidney function had worsened. The ER nurse told me that. After he heard about her supposed prognosis, Dr. Brightmore insisted she be admitted. No one argues with Dr. Brightmore."

"Because he was a pharmacist and is well-known in town?" Elrik asked.

Pauline shook her head. "Because he's on the hospital board. No one messes with board members, not if they want to keep their jobs."

"You're saying she didn't need to be admitted?" Elrik asked. "I thought her kidney function had worsened, that she'll soon need dialysis."

Pauline shrugged. "Not right now. I'm not saying her kidney won't get worse, but she's nowhere close to needing dialysis and certainly not from the Xylitol poisoning." She glanced around again. "But I didn't tell you that. I did not discuss a patient, certainly not the health of the girlfriend of a board member. I was just casually educating you about kidney disease and using a hypothetical patient while I did it."

"Why tell us this at all?" I asked.

"You were crying, and I felt bad. To me, the whole situation sounded manipulative. I saw you here, and I'm spontaneous. I thought you'd want to know."

With that, she scooted around us and raced down the sidewalk. When she reached the crosswalk, she bolted toward the parking lot on the opposite side.

"Well," I said, leaning against the window. "What do we make of this?"

Elrik leaned close. "It sounds like Sue has been lying about her health. The big question is, why?"

"Do you think Alfred knows? It didn't sound like he does. He was concerned about her and was urging her to consider dialysis."

"Which she isn't because she doesn't need it."

"Not yet. You heard Pauline. Her condition could worsen, and she might one day need it. She'll still refuse, I suspect."

"Maybe she said her condition had worsened to get sympathy. People do odd things for all sorts of reasons."

"How does this relate to Grannie, if at all?"

"No idea. I'll think about it and see if I can come up with some reasons."

"Sympathy's the only reason I can think of right now. Sue has always been someone who likes to talk about this or that joint aching, even her bowels, and what she takes to stay regular. Her knee that needs replacement. The pink spot on her face that may or may not be early skin cancer. Grannie talks about her health sometimes too. It might be an older person thing and not anything specific to Sue."

"Let me text her and see if I can stop by later today. I want to get to the bottom of this right away."

Did Sue have a reason to put the Xylitol in the punch? If she was looking for sympathy, that would be one way to do it, especially if she knew she'd be treated so well at the hospital. People had done worse things for attention.

He sent the text. After putting his phone away, he frowned at me. We needed to go see Hazel, but we still had a few minutes before she expected us to arrive.

"Let's run through this," I said. "Who are our primary suspects?"

We sat on the iron chairs, and he filled me in on his conversation with Ginny and Bob. Then he pulled out his phone to go through his list.

"Alfred could've done it to harm Sue," I said. "Hoping she'd go into full kidney failure, refuse dialysis and die, and he'd inherit her life insurance payout. He doesn't appear to know she's perfectly fine." That really was a sucky thing to do to someone who cared for you, and I wasn't sure what I thought about it. We'd all been worried about her.

"Sue also has a motive," Elrik said.

I couldn't think of why she'd do something like that to her best friend.

"Jealousy," Elrik offered. "She was winning the local awards until Grannie started knitting mittens."

"There's no way the committee will give the award to Grannie this year if she's on trial for poisoning her friends, let alone in jail."

"And Sue may know that the Xylitol wouldn't cause much harm if she was treated right away. She might've been willing to risk it."

I shook my head. "I still can't believe she'd do something like that. And why lie about her kidney disease?"

"Sympathy could sway the committee into giving the award to her instead of your grandmother."

Perhaps. "Who else could've done it?"

"Bob. He asked Grannie out, and she turned him down."

"My grandmother was quite the catch," I said with a laugh. "It seems like all the eligible bachelors in town asked her out. Bob has very limited mobility, and you said he arrived last."

"He's very low on the list."

"Who else?"

"We still need to talk to Hazel." He frowned at his phone. "Carla's the last suspect." His gaze met mine. "What does she stand to gain if your grandmother goes to jail?"

"I don't think she'd gain anything."

"What if she thought *you'd* be accused of putting the Xylitol in the punch?" he asked. "What would she gain if you went to jail?"

"The ice cream place would close. Grannie might let Carla rent the space instead. But she seems to have enough to deal with right now with Walter's properties. I doubt she has the capital to open an art studio even if the space was available. She'd have to renovate, and opening the studio doesn't guarantee sales. It takes time to build clientele and a reputation."

"We'll keep her on the list, however." He stood. "We should go speak with Hazel. Maybe she'll give us more clues."

"Or reveal that she's the one who did it," I said, though I was joking.

He tucked his phone into his back pocket. "What would be her motive?"

"If I went to jail, she could expand into my place and start offering yoga."

"We'll ask her about that."

We walked toward the entrance, and I was grateful we passed two families talking about getting ice cream. There was no mention of poison, no talk of bad reviews. This was going to be okay, thanks to the PR company's efforts. I wasn't even worried about the bill they'd send. They were worth almost any cost.

We stepped inside Boogey Beasts, where the elegance of ballet merged with the gritty strength of pole dancing.

The place was empty, but Hazel's office was in the back.

"No classes going right now," Elrik said softly.

"The place fills up after school and is busy well into the evening. She runs small and private classes in the morning. She has two instructors working with her as well. She's popular; people and monsters come quite a distance just to work with her."

"Going from ballet to stockbroker to pole dancing instructor is quite a switch."

I frowned, trying to remember. "I think her dad worked as a stockbroker. I doubt she started trading right away but with his connections, I bet she was able to land a sweet job that let her work her way up. She's retired from that now, of course. She comes from old money. Her dad owned real estate in New York City. A few buildings, I think."

The polished wooden floors shone under the soft lights recessed into the ceiling. Full-length mirrors covered the left wall from corner to corner, reflecting a row of classical barres worn smooth by countless fingertips and wrapped in tape at intervals for grip.

"Have you ever taken ballet?" Elrik asked, studying the room.

"Nope. Just those few pole classes where I spent more time on my ass than clinging to the pole. It takes time, and I just didn't have the patience." I waved toward the opening in the back of the room. "Hazel's office is that way."

We walked across the big open room, our footsteps echoing around us.

On the right, an arched entry led to the room where Hazel taught pole dancing. Sleek metal poles anchored securely from floor to ceiling at measured distances spanned the room.

A light floral aroma mingled with a hint of old sweat and rosin ballerinas dusted on their slippers for pointe work. Speakers perched in corners would soon vibrate with whatever music fit the class, from classic symphonies for ballet to the pulsing beats Hazel often used for her pole classes.

Exiting the studio, we turned right and started down the hall.

A guttural cry rang out ahead of us.

We shared a wide-eyed look before we rushed in that direction.

22

ELRIK

We reached the open office doorway at the same time and burst into the room, finding no one there.

An antique wooden desk had been placed halfway between the door and a bank of windows that looked out at a parking lot and straggly woods beyond.

A moan rang out from the other side of the desk, and we hurried that way, rounding the heavy wooden piece of furniture and coming to a stop.

"Hazel," Melly cried out, stooping down beside an elderly woman lying still on the floor.

Hazel wore a leotard with tights and a short skirt, and her long gray hair had been secured in a bun on the back of her head.

"Call 9-1-1," Melly said, stroking Hazel's forehead. "Hazel. Can you hear me?"

The older woman moaned and shifted on the floor. I called, and they said they'd send someone right away.

Hazel lay on her side with her legs curled up in a fetal

position. I didn't see any obvious injuries or blood, though a bruise was forming on her left temple. Had she hit her head when she fell or had something more suspicious occurred?

Melly looked up at me. "What do you think happened? She's not waking up." She placed her hand on Hazel's shoulder and lightly shook her. "Hazel? Hazel?"

The woman's eyes slowly opened. "Melly?"

"Yes, it's me, Melly. You're going to be okay. The ambulance is on the way."

"No ambulance." Hazel groaned and sat, leaning back against the wheeled chair. It promptly slipped toward the window, but Melly caught Hazel before she could fall to the floor again.

We eased her around until she could lean against her desk.

"You shouldn't be moving," Melly said. "Wait for the ambulance crew to take a look at you first."

"The day I stay on the floor is the day I die." Hazel peered up at me. "You're not an orc or an ogre."

"I'm an ice lord."

"What in the hell is an ice lord?"

My laugh snorted out. "Ice melts in hell." Or I assumed it did. I'd met a few demons, and each told me the stories were true. It was freakin' hot down there, wherever down there was.

"I see," Hazel said.

"What happened?" Melly asked, sitting on the floor beside Hazel.

"No, dear, don't do that. I need to get up." Hazel

looked back at me again. “You look like a strong male. Can you help me into my chair?”

“Of course.” I lifted her gently and placed her on the leather surface.

“Thanks.” She leaned back and closed her eyes, her hand rising to her left temple. “My head hurts.”

“Did you fall?” Melly got up and sat on the edge of the desk.

I stood to the side, ready to assist Hazel again if she needed me.

“The first thing I need you to do is call 9-1-1 and tell them to turn that ambulance around and take it back to the garage,” Hazel said, her voice getting stronger by the second. “I’m not going to the hospital.”

“You’ve got a bruise on your temple. You hit your head,” Melly said. “I’m sure you need to be examined.”

“Ah, yes.” Hazel frowned at me. “You’re Elrik, one of the new employees working at Monsters, PI. You were coming here today to ask me some questions. I remember now.”

“Questions can wait,” I said.

“Melly, call 9-1-1, if you please.” Hazel’s gaze didn’t leave me. “Ask your questions. I’ll do my best to answer. Then I can go lay down.”

“There’s no rush,” I said again. “Truly. Let’s make sure you’re okay before we do anything else.”

“Life’s too short to waste even a second. Questions,” Hazel growled.

I nodded to Melly who was holding up her phone, though she hadn’t yet dialed. She stepped out of the office and placed the call. I could hear her telling them

Hazel appeared okay, that Melly would try to convince her to be seen by a doctor, but for now, we didn't need an ambulance. Thanks, and all that.

She stepped back into the office and dragged a chair over from near the wall, placing it beside Hazel's. Sitting, she took Hazel's hand. "Tell us what happened. You've got a nasty bruise on your forehead."

"I have seizures," Hazel said, her shoulders drooping. "I've had them since the head injury I got when I fell all those years ago. My doctor has been playing with my medication again. He says there are drugs I can take with less side effects than the ones that have worked well forever. But now I'm having seizures again, so I'll have to call him and ask for another adjustment." She placed her hand on Melly's leg. "Please don't tell your grandmother. She'll be worried, and she has enough to deal with right now. I'm fine. I promise I won't drive. I can take a cab to and from work until I'm seizure-free long enough to get permission from my doctor to sit behind the wheel again."

"Does Grannie know about your seizures?" Melly asked.

"I don't believe I've mentioned it to her. There has been no need. It's part of my past, and other than the joy I take from teaching dance, I prefer to forget that I had so much potential long ago." She sighed. "Potential that was lost when I fell. As for my seizures, they've been well controlled for years. Once I'm on the right meds again, it won't matter." She lifted her eyebrows my way. "What questions do you have?"

"I wanted to ask you about the church social and the Xylitol poisoning," I said.

"That was the first time in my life I've had my stomach pumped, and let me tell you, it's not pleasant having a tube shoved into your nose and down your throat to your stomach. At least it was quick."

Melly squeezed her hand.

"Could you tell me exactly what happened from the moment you arrived?" I asked.

"Sure." Hazel frowned. "I got there at the same time as Carla. Sue, Alfred, and Bob were already there."

"I've questioned Bob," I said with a frown. "He said he was the last to arrive."

"My brain may be fuzzy after a seizure, but I'm otherwise sharp," she said. "He was there when I walked in the door. He said I was silly wearing a jacket when it was seventy outside, but I get cold easily, and it's not like it hurts anyone else if I wear it. Seeing that Rose wasn't around, I asked about her, because I could see someone had already made her punch." Her gaze fell on Melly. "You didn't."

"No. Grannie felt well enough to make it that night," Melly said. "After she finished, she went to the bathroom."

"That's what Sue told me." Hazel rubbed her face. "I put my crockpot with beef stew on the table and went to the bathroom, knocking on the door and asking if Rose needed help. She did, so I went inside. She'd left her walker outside the stall and asked me to bring it with her. I pointed out that there wasn't much room and with the door open, anyone entering might see her sitting on the toilet. She said she didn't care about anything like that."

For a woman who was worried about how she was seen in the community, that was odd, but Rose was assertive. If she decided she wanted her walker in the stall with her, she wouldn't care if anyone saw her.

"She didn't use the handicap stall?" Melly asked.

Hazel's nose twisted. "Someone plugged it up and it reeked in there. I'm sure the janitor has taken care of it by now."

"I'm sure they have," I said.

"After that," Hazel said, "Rose shooed me out, saying she could handle hiking up her underwear and returning to the main room on her own. I went back to the others. They'd already gotten into the punch."

"Not Bob," I said.

"He doesn't like it. He was still parked near the wall where someone had left him. He called out to me, asking for help getting over to the table. Said his scooter was having battery issues. If Ginny hadn't stopped by and brought a new battery, he would've been stuck near the wall all evening. There's no lift there like in his home."

"Ginny stopped by?" Melly asked, her gaze meeting mine. "Wasn't she sitting in the van in case he needed her?"

"I'm just telling you what I heard," Hazel said. "He said he'd called her, and she was coming right away with a new battery."

"She must've been sitting in the van, then," Melly said.

Hazel shrugged. “I guess so. Ginny put the new battery in his scooter and left.”

“To wait in the van?” I asked.

“I assume so.”

“Bob said he didn’t drink any punch,” I said. “That he doesn’t like it.”

Hazel shrugged. “I’ve seen him drink it in the past, but maybe he’s tired of it now. It’s sweet, though it was extra sweet that night. Sue, Alfred, and Carla were already on their second or third cups. The punchbowl was half empty! Damn, they’re greedy, sucking it down before the rest of us could get some.” Her husky laugh rang out. “I hurried over because I didn’t want to miss out. But I’d only started my second cup when Sue began vomiting. She keeled over onto the floor and Alfred stooped down beside her. It got pretty frantic about then. My belly was rolling, and I wanted to help Sue, but I barely made it to the trash can myself.”

“Where was Rose by then?”

“I could hear her walker making clunking sounds in the hall. She joined us after I’d finished at the barrel.”

“Why did they pump your stomach if you threw up the punch?” I asked.

She shrugged. “I guess they wanted to make sure it was all gone. At that time, no one knew what was going on other than that a bunch of us were getting violently ill. Suspecting something horrible, they may have decided it was safer to make sure none of us retained even a bit of whatever was making us sick.”

“Meanwhile, Bob was sitting in his chair, watching all of this unfold?” Melly asked.

Hazel frowned. "I was still hovering by the bucket, but I believe I remember seeing him closer to the table, though on the food end. He wasn't near the punch, and he didn't have a drink or food in his hands. At least he didn't have to have his stomach pumped. Ginny came back in with the ambulance crew, who Bob wisely called right away. We knew something terrible was going on, and we needed help."

"The ambulance came quickly," I said.

"Three of them because there were six of us there. They didn't have to take Rose, Ginny, or Bob to the hospital since they hadn't eaten or drunk anything, though they checked them out in case it was a gas leak in the kitchen or something like that. Detective Carter ruled that out quickly. At least we're all okay."

Except supposedly Sue. Had she shared her kidney problems with anyone but Alfred?

"Detective Carter must've been nearby, on patrol or something," Hazel said. "The ambulance driver notified him, and he arrived at the same time they did. Since we'd only had the punch and hadn't gotten into the food, and Rose made the punch, she was taken to the station for questioning. The rest of us went to the hospital to be examined."

"Except Bob and Ginny."

"He refused. Ginny loaded him into the van, and you should've seen the glare she sent Rose."

"She blamed Rose?" I asked.

"It appeared so. The van peeled out of the parking lot a short time after that. I just don't get it. It's not like Rose to hurt others."

"You and she have been friends for a long time," I said.

"Yes, I'm practically Melly's godmother, though that's not official." She patted Melly's leg. "I wasn't there when you were born, but I've been around while you were growing up. We're all quite proud of our Melly."

"She's very special." I grinned her way.

Hazel crooked her head to look up at me. "Are you single, Elrik?"

"More or less." Now that Melly was in my life? No.

"That's not a true answer, but I'm not going to press you." Hazel's laugh rang out. "As for Ginny, I guess she has enough reason to be upset with Rose."

"Because she slipped and broke her hip at the function hall?" Melly said.

"Sure, but Rose stated right away she had no interest in suing. Ginny's quite protective of that insurance business."

Melly shifted on her chair. "She's helping Bob."

"Is that what she said?" Hazel frowned. "Helping? More like trying to steal the business right out from underneath him."

23

MELLY

"What do you mean by that?" I asked Hazel. Ginny had always come across to me as if she cared about Bob, that he was more than just a job. She used to visit him even before his health started to fail. When he started having a hard time getting around, she'd moved in with him and taken care of all his needs. Bob hadn't acted as if he was worried about Ginny trying to steal anything from him. But would he? He might not know.

"She keeps trying to get him to sign the business over to her," Hazel said.

So he did know.

Elrik frowned. "Maybe he's okay with that."

"Maybe he is and maybe he isn't," Hazel said. "But he built that business into what it is today with a lot of hard work. Long hours that ruined his marriage."

"He's divorced?" Elrik asked.

"At least forty years ago. She moved away, and I'm not sure he's heard from her since."

"Does he have children to inherit his business?" I asked.

Hazel shook her head. "They didn't have any. He never remarried—except to his career, I suppose. He was working long days right up until he started to get sicker. That's when Ginny moved in and started trying to take control of everything."

"He might be willing to hand it over to her since he can't do it himself any longer," I said. "He's past retirement age."

"That man will never retire." Hazel grunted. "Rose chewed Ginny out more than once, telling her to stop trying to steal his business, that if she wanted it, she could buy it just like anyone else would."

"Why would my grandmother get into the middle of that?" I asked with concern. "She rarely butts into anyone else's business."

"She's always been protective of Bob. However, I believe Ginny's help is the only reason he's able to remain in his home, and I give her credit for that. I don't hear him complaining about her handling the business end of things either, and I'm sure he'd voice concerns if he had them." She huffed. "I told Rose that myself, told her to leave it to Bob and Ginny to figure out between themselves."

"My grandmother can be quite protective," I said.

Hazel nodded slowly. "She turned down his marriage proposal, but I think she still has some feelings for him."

I gulped. "Marriage proposal?"

Hazel patted my leg again. "This was a long time ago. You were fifteen? Sixteen? About that age. Rose told me about it. He's much younger than her by at least fourteen years. She liked him quite a bit, but she couldn't see how it could work with the age gap. She also confided to me that while she cared for him, she wasn't interested in being married to someone who was already married to their job. Bob was that devoted to building his business."

"Is his business worth much?" I asked. "If he couldn't manage it any longer, it would close. If Ginny's keeping it going, then he has income from that."

"I imagine you're right. I think everyone in this town and all the surrounding ones pay premiums to Sterling for one kind of policy or another. Even I have life insurance, liability for my business, plus policies for my home and auto with Sterling. Believe me, that business is solid."

If anyone in town would know something like that, it would be Hazel.

I still couldn't get over the fact that my grandmother had considered marrying Bob. "Do you think she turned him down because of me?"

"Never that. I'm sure she would've welcomed the help raising you, though you were a sweet child. Never a bother to anyone."

That made me feel better.

I sensed we were running out of questions. When I glanced Elrik's way, he nodded, telling me he'd pretty much read my mind.

I stood, gazing down at Hazel. "What can I do for you?"

"Nothing," she said, gently touching her forehead. "I need to get up and get moving. I have classes to teach this evening."

"Can't someone else handle them for you? I'm worried about you." She could have another seizure and be seriously injured.

"That's not a bad idea." She lifted her phone. "I'll call Judy and see if she'll cover tonight. She was just saying she needed more hours."

"Then we can take you home."

She shook her head. "No, you go on. I'll wait here for Judy. My first class doesn't start for an hour, and I'm sure she'll be willing to drive me home once she gets here. I'll lay down and rest. I promise."

I stood. "You're sure I can't get you anything? Maybe a glass of water or a bag of ice for your head?"

"I'm fine." She rose, and I could see she was steady. Her eyes were clear too. "I'll call my doctor first thing in the morning and tell him I want to go back on my old meds. They work when this new medication doesn't." She strode around the desk, and I was grateful to see she appeared to be back to her old self. "Let me walk you to the door."

I shared a look with Elrik, but we both shrugged. We couldn't make her accept our help, and I could understand her need for independence.

We followed her to the door, which she opened.

A troll family was passing on the sidewalk. The young daughter peered in through the opening, a big grin on her green face.

"Dance," she cried, her eyes bright with excitement. "Dancing."

"Tomorrow, Tria," Hazel said with a wave. "I'll see you tomorrow morning."

"If I think of anything else, I'll give you a call," she said to me. "I want to do all I can to help you clear Rose's name. She's a special woman, and she doesn't deserve this."

"Thank you." I gave her a hug, then held her forearms, staring into her eyes. "Are you sure you don't need anything from us?"

"I'm doing alright." Hazel's smile rose, and she was just as pretty today as she'd been when she did ballet. She'd shown me pictures multiple times over the years, and the best ones hung in her office.

We stepped out onto the sidewalk.

"You talked with Sue, right?" Hazel asked.

"We did. Bob too. Carla, Ginny, and Alfred. Everyone who was there that evening."

"Good, good," Hazel said. "Did Sue tell you why she was hovering around the punch bowl but then raced out to her vehicle?"

24

ELRIK

"She didn't mention anything like that," Melly said, her concerned gaze meeting mine.

"While I was lying on that hospital stretcher with that tube up my nose, I started thinking," Hazel said. "Sue was near the punchbowl but then she left the building. When she came back, she started chugging the punch like she'd run a marathon without taking one sip of water."

"You're pretty close. She and Alfred went on a long hike," I said. "She told us they finished late, that they *hadn't* brought water, and that when they got here, she was very thirsty."

"Sue never does anything like that," Hazel said. "She's told me a number of times that she's supposed to take in regular fluids, that it's good for her kidneys. I can't believe she'd go for a hike without water."

I couldn't see how this might play into her possibly poisoning the punch, but it wouldn't hurt to ask her why she'd left the building abruptly.

Melly's gaze met mine. "Do we have any other questions?"

I shook my head. "Thank you," I told Hazel.

"You're welcome. I'll see you two around?" Hazel's gaze traveled back and forth between us.

Melly kissed Hazel's cheek. "Take care. I'll call you later to make sure you don't need anything."

"You're a sweet girl, Melly." Hazel stepped inside and started shutting the door. "Come visit me anytime."

We started walking toward Creature Cones.

I looked at my phone. No return text from Sue.

"I'll ask Sue about where she went when she has time to talk," I said as we stopped outside the ice cream shop. Customers had lined up in front of the counter, and that would please Melly.

"Let me know what she says?"

"I will." I stroked her face. "What would you like to do tonight after dinner?"

She gave me a sly smile. "You mentioned something about ice?"

"Yes, I did. Tonight."

She leaned into my chest and gazed up at me. "What sort of icy thing are you planning, my spicy, icy lord?"

I laughed and gave her a quick kiss, wishing we had time for more. "You'll see."

"Or feel." She winked before she sauntered inside.

Grinning, I watched her for a moment before I turned and strode across the road, aiming for my truck. Inside, I called Sue, who answered and said she had a few minutes to talk if I came over now. After parking in her driveway, I walked up the path to the light green painted cottage placed near the woods. Flowers overflowed the window boxes and the well-tended, narrow strips of garden along the path.

She opened the front door before I could knock. “Come on in, Elrik.” Inside, she took me into her kitchen. “Would you like some coffee?”

“No thank you.” I sat at the island while she fixed a cup for herself and brought it over, remaining standing. She added cream and sipped, placing her mug back on the counter after.

“How are you feeling?” I asked, noting a pile of papers and a manilla envelope labeled Sterling on the end of the island. Did it contain the beneficiary papers I’d seen at the hospital?

“I feel wonderful.” Her bright smile made her green eyes sparkle. “I’m much better.”

“I’m sorry about the progression of your disease.” This wasn’t the most delicate way to put it, but I wasn’t sure how else to bring this up without revealing that the nurse had shared confidential information.

“Thank you.”

“Melly’s really worried about you. She said you’re like a second grandmother to her.”

Her smile faded, and her gaze dropped from mine. “Yes.”

“You’re sure you won’t consider dialysis?”

She started pacing back and forth in the kitchen, her shoes squeaking on the linoleum. “My dad hated it. I always told myself I wouldn’t put myself through it.”

“I understand. Melly does too.”

“A lot of patients do fine with it, but it made him

horribly sick. He'd lay in bed all the next day, and then it was time to do it all over again the day after that."

"Your wishes are important. The quality of your life is important."

"Quality," she huffed.

"It's hard to lose someone you care about, but I know Melly understands. She'll support you no matter what you choose to do."

"Melly's amazing." Pausing in the middle of the kitchen, she cupped her face. When she lowered her hands back to her sides, her sorrow-filled gaze met mine. "I shouldn't. I can't."

"Can't what?"

With a shake of her head, she strode back over to the counter, leaning her arms on it.

"Can I confess something to you?" she whispered.

"Of course."

I said nothing, waiting to see what she'd say. Would she confess to dumping Xylitol into the punch to gain sympathy?

"My kidney is fine," she said in a rush.

"Really?" I tried to act surprised, but I wasn't much of an actor.

"I fibbed."

Now there was a word appropriate for an elementary school teacher.

"What do you mean?" I asked.

"Alfred and I got married a few months ago. I haven't told Melly yet, but Rose knows."

Rose hadn't mentioned that to us.

"I swore her to secrecy," Sue said before I could voice

my thoughts. "We plan to announce it soon, but . . ." She fiddled with the handle of her mug, running her fingers up and down the smooth surface. "Alfred's younger than me. I know I shouldn't worry about something like that, but I do. So . . . When I was hospitalized, I told him my kidney disease is advancing. It's not. The doctor said the Xylitol made no difference."

How could she hope to hold onto someone she loved with lies? "You should confess to Alfred, not me."

"I know I should but once I started telling fibs, they got tangled together, and I can't find a way out of them."

"Confess everything."

"I know I should, but it's hard."

"Did you put Xylitol in the punch?"

Horror filled her eyes, and she reeled away from me. "I might tell a fib about my kidney disease, but I would never purposefully do something like that to myself or anyone else. It would be stupid. I could truly damage my kidney."

Yet she'd lie about it to someone she supposedly loved. I wasn't ruling her out yet. "Have you shared this with Rose? She's worried about you. Melly is too."

"I plan to. Soon. When Alfred kissed that woman . . . Actually, *she* kissed him, not the other way around. I see that now. He loves me. He's made that plain."

I didn't point out that he'd explain something like that away if he was trying to get Sue to name him her life insurance beneficiary.

"I thought I could hold onto my younger husband with sympathy," Sue said. "But that's a mean thing to do when you're trying to save your marriage. I'm going to tell him tonight. I hope he'll forgive me." She gave me a sad smile. "That's why I didn't hesitate to sign the paperwork he brought to the hospital. I have a rather large life insurance policy I've paid into for most of my life. He suggested I name him as the beneficiary not long after we got married, but I balked at first. After what happened at the social club, and seeing how concerned he was about me, I decided to show him I trust him and sign."

Interesting that Alfred had been urging her to sign since they married.

"Who do you think put Xylitol in the punch?" I asked.

"I'm not sure. After I got there, and I'd helped Rose into the bathroom, I realized I'd forgotten the coleslaw I put all that effort into making. Alfred and I went out to get it together."

That explained why she'd left.

"Let's go through the timeframe once more," I said. "You arrived and almost immediately helped Rose to the bathroom?"

"Yes. Alfred helped too, though he didn't go inside the stall. We initially waited in the hallway. I wanted to be there to be with her until she'd returned to the function room. She does very well with the walker, but it can snag on things. I'm sure she won't need it much longer, but I didn't want her to fall again. I could hear someone else arriving, but I couldn't see who it was."

Was that when the punch was poisoned?

"You know how mayonnaise can go bad if it's not refrigerated? I always put a bowl of ice beneath my coleslaw to keep it cold. I told Rose I'd left it in the car, and she insisted I go get it right away. Alfred came with me. He's trying to quit, but it's hard, you know?"

"Quit?"

"He's smoked for most of his life. I keep telling him it's going to ruin his lungs. He finally agreed. He's cut back to one cigarette a day. He takes a few puffs, carefully puts it out, then saves the rest for later. Next week, he's cutting back to half a cigarette a day. He used to smoke a pack, which I just can't imagine, but we thought a slow wean like this might be easier than going cold turkey."

"You're saying Alfred was with you from the time you arrived until you came back inside and started drinking the punch?"

"Yes. He stood by the car and took his two puffs while I grabbed the coleslaw from the backseat." She winced. "I have another confession to make. We . . . didn't go back inside right away."

I frowned. "Why not?"

"We . . ." Color rose in her cheeks. "We haven't been married long. We're practically newlyweds. We, um, got into the backseat and . . . I don't want to say any more."

I held in my laugh. "You don't need to. How long do you think it was before you went back inside?"

"Quite a long time. Alfred's a young man compared to me."

I really didn't want to hear about his stamina in bed, but I did need to know the timeframe.

"I'd say ten minutes," she added.

I didn't comment on the fact that ten minutes from start to finish was not anything to crow about.

"I heard other vehicles arriving, car doors closing,"

she said. Blinking slowly, she stared forward, remembering that evening. "Anyway. We finished and went inside. I made a beeline for the punch, as I always do. As I said, we'd hiked, and I was very thirsty."

"With kidney disease, I'd think you'd carry water with you everywhere." By mentioning it this way, I wasn't bringing in what Hazel said.

"I usually do, but the hike was spontaneous. Alfred was quite insistent, and I really don't want to disappoint my new husband. My kidney is fine. The hospital ran all sorts of tests and told me I was doing great when Alfred wasn't in the room. I asked them not to share my medical condition with my boyfriend. That's what the community thinks he is, and we agreed to call him that while he was there."

"Why?"

"Because we're still planning our reception. We don't want anyone to know until the announcements go out."

I guessed that made sense. "Where was Rose when you went back inside?"

"Still in the bathroom."

"Were you concerned that she was taking that long?" Ten minutes was a long time even for someone using a walker.

"Not really. She said she had to," Sue coughed and lowered her voice, "poop. I wasn't going to get involved with that. By then, I was more worried about everyone crowding around the punchbowl, scooping it out. It goes fast."

"Who else was in the function hall by then?" We were missing something. I just couldn't determine what.

"Bob. Hazel. And Carla."

"Did you happen to see Ginny there?"

"No, but Bob was all set up in this chair, so I assume she was out in the van like usual."

"Did you notice if the van was there when you were out front?"

"It was." She took a sip of her coffee before placing the mug back on the counter. "It's big. Silver. They park in the handicap spot right out front, and you can't miss it."

"Was she in it?"

"I didn't look."

That didn't mean she wasn't there. "Did Bob drink any punch?"

"I don't think so. He usually sticks to ginger ale. He drove his scooter over to the buffet table while I was sipping my first cup. He loves Carla's barbecued mini weenies, and they go almost as fast as Rose's punch."

"What does he do after dishing up a plate?"

"He always places it on his lap and steers his scooter over to the table. We leave a spot without a chair and his scooter fits nicely beneath the table. I finished my second glass of punch and poured my third. Feeling bad for Bob because it was nearly gone, I got a cup for him and brought it to the table in case he wanted some."

"Did he drink any?"

"I don't know. I just grabbed my third cup. It had been hot all day, and I was thirsty. Between the four of us, we were close to emptying the punch bowl. I started vomiting soon after, and honestly, I don't recall much of what happened after that. I was too focused on making sure my vomit reached the inside of the trash barrel and didn't splatter on the floor."

Since I couldn't think of anything else to ask, I stood. "Thank you very much for speaking with me."

"You're most welcome."

"I hope you're able to straighten things out with Alfred."

She fidgeted with her coffee cup, sloshing the liquid around. "I hope so too."

As I drove back toward town, I pretty much crossed Sue off as a suspect.

That left Hazel, Alfred, Carla, Bob, and Ginny, with Alfred at the top of the list.

25

MELLY

By the time I closed for the afternoon, I was feeling much better about my business. We were busy with customers all afternoon and there had been no repeat of the one-star trolling on the town website.

Elrik had called and filled me in on his conversation with Sue. Like him, I suspected she hadn't dumped the Xylitol into the punch.

Who had and why?

Elrik sent me a text as I was getting into my car. *I'm about to place the order for our meal at Kraken's Keep. Have you thought of anything in particular you or Grannie would like?*

Nope. Surprise us.

Alright, I will. After we've eaten and she's settled, we can follow through on my icy plan.

I can't wait.

As I drove home, I turned up the radio and sang along

with the tune, only lowering the volume when I pulled into the driveway.

"Well, well, I'm glad you're here," Grannie said as I stepped inside her kitchen. She sat at the table with a cup of tea but rose to her feet and flung her arms up in the air. "Surprise."

"Where's your walker?" I asked, not seeing it in the kitchen.

"I'm done with it." A big smile rose on her face. "The physical therapist said I could use a cane now. I've graduated, and it's about time."

"It hasn't been that long." I crossed the room and kissed her cheek. "This is amazing! We need to celebrate. Good thing Elrik's bringing dinner."

"He's such a sweet man." When she looked up at me, her hazel eyes sparkled. "I don't want to pry, but I can tell you have feelings for him."

"I think I'm falling in love with him, Grannie." My grin made my cheeks ache. "He seems to feel the same way."

"Wonderful." Grannie clapped her hands. "Do you think he'll propose?"

"We're nowhere near talking about something like that." But would we get there? I suspected we could.

All we needed to do was figure out who tried to frame Grannie and then we could put this behind us and . . . Who knew where things would go between Elrik and I after that?

"How's the investigation going?" she asked as she settled at the table again.

I sat across from her.

We'd already decided not to share too much with my grandmother. She was under enough stress as it was. No need to add to that. I did tell her I knew about Sue and Alfred's marriage.

"She swore me to secrecy after they returned from Vegas." Grannie sipped her tea before placing the cup back in the saucer with a clink.

"Why keep it a secret?" Would Grannie's reason match Sue's?

"Alfred felt he should notify his family first."

Not the same answer, but also not far off. Invitations to a reception could include notification.

"He must've done that by now," I said.

"He sure did. Sue told me he had. A few were upset, of course, so he wanted to give them time to adjust before the news spread through town."

"Why would they be upset?"

"Alfred's very wealthy. Old money. His distant relatives hobnobbed with the Vanderbilts. I know for a fact that Alfred not only has a gorgeous home in Kennebunkport, Maine, he has a villa in the mountains of Italy, plus he owns a complete island in the Caribbean with staff, a big boat parked at a dock, you name it. The works. Now that he and Sue are married, he's made it clear she'll inherit it all. He'd never married prior to Sue, and he has no children, so I'm sure some of his relatives believed they'd benefit once he'd passed, which, sadly, will happen soon."

I frowned. "What do you mean?"

"Didn't you know? He has terminal cancer."

Oh, my. Did Sue know this? She must. I could understand why she might not have shared it with Elrik, however. Not without Alfred's permission, though she'd told my grandmother. Or someone had.

But Alfred had definitely not tried to kill Sue to inherit her life insurance money. He not only didn't need it, but he also wouldn't be able to spend it.

I hated where this thought led me.

He and Sue were squabbling at the hospital, and he'd stated she talked him into the marriage.

What if Sue had dumped the Xylitol into the punch to speed up Alfred's demise?

26

ELRIK

I ordered and then picked up dinner from Kraken's Keep, and we sat at a table in the backyard shelling our lobsters and dipping the succulent pieces into bowls of butter, accompanying it with garlic rolls, corn on the cob, and twice baked potatoes.

After, we went inside with Grannie Rose and took care of the dishes.

"You really don't need to keep doing all these things for me," Rose said after Melly mentioned laying out her pills and getting a new glass for water. "I'm mobile now that I have Fredrick."

Melly's eyebrows lifted. "Frederick?"

Grannie hefted her cane and shook it, her eyes sparkling. "My new dance partner. He's quite polite and helpful. The point is, I don't need help any longer. You two go have fun together." She winked my way. "I can take care of things from now on, Melly, though I greatly appreciate your help when I couldn't do it for myself."

"We'll still have meals together," Melly said with a

touch of sadness, closing the dishwasher and starting it. "Right?"

Rose chuckled. "You're a wonderful cook and with Elrik here bringing us lobster, I'd be a fool to turn that down."

"You're sure?" Melly asked. "I'll just set things up for your dentures. Put out your nightie. You can—"

"Melly." A hint of warning came through in Rose's voice. "I can do this. I know the time is coming when I'll need you to do it for me forever, but for now, I want to handle it."

Melly sighed and gave Grannie Rose a hug. "Alright." When she looked my way, her eyes sparkled with tears. "I love you. I like doing things for you."

Rose patted Melly's back. "I love you too, honey. But I want you to enjoy your evening with Elrik. Don't worry about me."

Melly stepped back and crimped her lips together, blinking fast to dispel the tears. "I'll check in before I go to bed. Keep your phone nearby."

"I will." Rose patted her pocket. "I charged it this morning, so it's nice and juicy." She waved toward the door. "Go. Lock up for me, would you?"

We stepped outside, and Melly tested the knob to ensure it was locked, before we walked down the back steps.

"I feel like a parent sending their child off to school for the first time. My little one is getting independent." Her low laugh rang out. "An eighty-year-old little one, but you know what I mean."

"You love her. You worry about her with good reason. But she's doing well. No more walker."

"The cane they left will be safer. I worried the walker would snag on a rug and she'd fall again, but she refused to let me take the rugs up and put them away."

"We'll check on her later, if you want."

"Thank you." She looked up at me. "What sort of icy treat do you have in store for me tonight?"

"Let's go to the beach, and I'll show you."

We walked down the sidewalk and like before, we left our sandals by the bench. The sun had set, and it was a clear night, the inky sky peppered with stars. Wispy clouds drifted across the half-moon that shed just enough light to see where we were walking.

"I'm very curious about this," she said. "I'm picturing a mini glacier with a crevasse we can climb down into."

"I wish I could show you that. Instead . . ." I waved toward the small table ahead I'd arranged to have Kraken's Keep deliver. Two chairs waited, and we sat. The staff who'd helped set things up nodded my way before turning to stride toward the restaurant.

Melly rapped her knuckles on the table with a clang. "This sounds like metal, not ice." Wiggling in her chair, she smiled. "My seat's not cold either."

"How about this?" I tugged the basket out from beneath the table and dropped it on my lap, setting glass dishes on the table and bottles of colorful syrup. A flick of my finger toward the table, and snow overflowed the bowls. Another nod, and a big ice sculpture appeared on the sand beside us.

Melly gasped and shot me a grin before rising and walking slowly around it. “It’s beautiful.”

I’d crafted a wave cresting, even included beads of ice clinging to the tip.

“A whale!” She pointed toward the sea below the long wave. “And dolphins. So pretty. How did you do it?”

“Some would say I used magic, but I’m an ice lord. Snow and ice respond to my command.”

“Wow.” Striding back over to the table, she sat again, looking down at her bowl of snow.

“This isn’t as impressive as the sculpture, but it’s tasty.” I pointed to the bottles. “Raspberry. Strawberry. Blueberry. And chocolate syrup. Your choice.”

“Maybe I want it all.”

I suspected she wasn’t only speaking of snow flavorings. “It’s yours. You just have to hold out your hand.”

She reached across the table, and I took her hand and kissed each of her knuckles.

“Thank you,” she said. “This is special.”

“You’re welcome. Only the best for you.”

We coated our snow and ate some while the sculpture melted. I hadn’t expected it to last long in this heat.

A few people stopped to admire it, their gazes gliding across us.

When we’d eaten our fill, we rose.

“The staff at Kraken’s Keep will take care of the table and the heat will melt the sculpture,” I said. “I have one more icy surprise.”

She looked up at me with so much happiness in her eyes, it humbled me. I still couldn’t believe this woman liked me, that she wanted to be with me.

"What is it?" she asked.

While waves swished up the shore and danced across our ankles, I snapped my fingers, and created an icicle about six inches long and an inch and a half thick. "For you." I held it out with a smile.

"That's . . . amazing."

"That's me. Amazing." My low laugh rang out.

Her smile grew sly. "Your icicle is rather phallic looking. Is that the point?"

A low hum ran through my bones, and my cock stirred, sensing action. Leaning close, I whispered by her ear. "Suck on it for me, would you? I want to watch."

Her eyes widened as she took it from me. "It's cold." A quiver went through her. As she held it, water trickled down her arm, falling to the sand.

"Suck on my ice cock," I said softly. "If you do a good job, I'll let you suck on something else after."

"This . . . This . . ." Her breathing came out in startled gasps.

The heat pouring through me would melt a glacier. "I have all sorts of ideas for things we can do with ice."

"I'm sure you do." Her swallow took a long time to go down.

"It's melting."

"So it is." After shooting me a mischievous smile, she lifted the icicle. At first, she was tentative, barely taking the tip into her mouth.

"It's cold," she said.

"*Icy*."

"At least your cock isn't this cold because . . ."

"What if it could be?"

Her breath caught. "Not this cold. That would be . . ."

I kissed her cheek. "I can adjust the temperature."

"Why didn't you do that the first time we were together?"

"I didn't want to scare you away."

"Elrik. This is an incredible turn-on. You know that, right?"

My grin made my face ache. "I was hoping it would be."

"No frostbite down there, however," she warned.

"No frostbite. I swear."

She sucked more of the icicle into her mouth and swept her tongue across the tip.

My groan ripped out.

Her eyes sparkling, she pumped the icicle in and out of her mouth, taking more of it than I'd expected.

"Tastes good," she mumbled. "Spicy."

"Plain ice is boring, don't you think?"

She pulled the icicle out of her mouth with a pop. "You're right. I still can't believe you can snap your fingers and create ice." With a hum, she sucked the icicle back into her mouth.

She worked it well, and my poor cock turned into a rod in my pants. I kept picturing tugging the icicle from her mouth and replacing it with my cock. Her lips and tongue would be cold on my overheated flesh.

I was breathing heavily, as if I'd been running.

She slid the icicle out of her mouth. "I want the real deal, Elrik." She took my hand and started running, dragging me down the beach.

I laughed as I kept up, not sure where she was going

but determined to follow this woman to the ends of the earth if that brought her joy.

Finally, she stopped in a section of the beach with dunes overgrown with grass. Only a few homes had been built in this area, and they sat well back from the shore.

Peering around, she pointed. “I can’t believe I’m even suggesting it, but there’s a park bench up there that’s shielded by beach grass and wild rose bushes. It’s quite isolated.”

“Lead away.”

After tossing the icicle aside, she took my hand and guided me up the shore and along a narrow, sandy path weaving through the dunes. The edges of the path were roped off to keep anyone from climbing the small hills overgrown with delicate vegetation. We walked out into a small open area where they’d placed a wooden bench. She guided me there and turned me to face her.

With a sultry smile, she undid my pants and tugged them down. “Sit, ice lord. It’s time I heated you up.”

27

MELLY

I'd never sucked on a guy's cock before Elrik. Never wanted to either. But since meeting him, everything had changed. I might be unsure about where our relationship was going, but I'd already proven I could give him pleasure. That empowered me in a way nothing else ever had.

Feeding me a sultry smile, he settled on the bench with his legs splayed wide and his gorgeous cock standing at attention. He was much taller than me, but sitting put him at human height, and because I was tall myself, I could kneel on the sand between his thighs and reach quite easily.

Leaning over his cock, I stared down at it while rubbing his thighs in slow circles. Each etched pattern brought my fingers closer. Closer. Until I touched the base.

He released a low groan, and his eyelids slid closed. He tipped his head back and gave himself over to me. I was in control of his pleasure, but this wasn't about anything like that. I wanted to do this for him, to hear him growl my name and shout when he came.

I held his cock in place and slid my tongue from the base to the tip. His body stilled, though his muscles tightened.

"Melly," he breathed, his words music to my ears alone. "You . . ."

My knees shook, and I melted from the way he said my name. It would be easy to tug him down to the sand, to take his cock and guide it inside me, but I wanted to do this. I sucked the head of his cock into my mouth. Yeah, he was big, and there was no way I could take all of him without practice, but I'd take all I could, just like I had the other night when we were first together.

His taste was as spicy as the icicle, like cinnamon combined with something that tingled across my tongue like hot chilis. I loved it. I wanted more.

Every bit of him was gorgeous, like he was a statue carved from ice who melted for me alone. The thought thrilled through me. I sensed my future only held happiness because he would share it with me.

My body tightened, and heat swirled through me, centering in my core. I wanted him. Craved him like no other. I couldn't wait to feel him deep inside me again.

His fingers slid through my hair, and as I moved my mouth up and down, taking him deeper with each of my thrusts, he cupped my head, holding me in place. His groans erupted around us.

I was lost in this moment; in the pleasure I was giving this man who'd quickly come to mean everything to me.

There wasn't anything better than knowing he was fully into this because *I* was the one doing it for him.

"Melly," he growled. "I can't . . . You shouldn't."

I wanted to. So much. I wanted him to come in my mouth. I'd suck it down like I did his cock right now, and I'd relish the notion that in this, he was mine.

I watched him while I slid my tongue up and down his length, and the pleasure on his face was my undoing. I shifted my knees, rubbing my thighs together, but the movement didn't quite tease the area where I ached for him the most.

He must've sensed my need, because he lifted me. While I whimpered and clung to his cock, he settled me on the bench beside him where I could still reach, but he could touch me. He bunched up my dress, and cool night air bathed my thighs and ass. He wrenched my underwear to the side and slid his fingers deeper.

"Wet. So wet for me." He drove a finger inside me, and my moan ripped up my throat. It was all I could do to focus on sucking his cock and swirling my tongue across the head.

Need made me jerk my hips back to meet his fingers. He added another, the stretch making me need him even more.

He kept plunging them inside me, then pulling them out, gliding them across my clit before pushing them all the way to the hilt.

"Melly," he growled. "I need you."

I released his cock only long enough to look up at him. "I'm yours."

"Climb on me, pretty one. Ride me until we scream out our joy."

I didn't need any more encouragement than that. I released his cock and stood in front of him, shimmying out of my underwear, leaving my dress on.

I climbed onto his lap, and he placed his hands on my hips as I settled myself over him.

It didn't take much to guide the head of his cock to my entrance, and it took even less effort on my part to let myself go and drop down onto his shaft. He filled me so completely that I wanted to weep.

No, I wanted to ride. I'd buck against this guy until we both shattered.

He curled his body forward and kissed me, his mouth searing across mine. But when I started moving, we couldn't maintain the kiss. We burst apart, sharing smiles that dissolved into moans.

My heart pounded as I moved faster, his hands on my hips lifting me and pushing me back down.

He slid one hand between us and stroked my clit. I nearly shot off right then and there. No, no, no. I wanted this to last all night long, not end in one big explosion now.

"Take me," he growled. "Claim my body in the way only you can."

Need coiled inside me, swirling down to make me even wetter. I started moving faster, my body jerking up and falling back down. Each time, he thrust his hips up to meet me.

As I moved, I yanked at his shirt. He paused only long enough to rip it up over his head and throw it aside. That gave me full access, and I kissed his chest, running my tongue across his nipple. It beaded, so I did it to the other one. I couldn't resist running my fingertips across his rippling muscles, tracing each one while I sucked on his nipple.

He urged me to go faster, driving up while I plunged down.

I cried out at the wonder. Nothing felt better than my ice lord pushing himself deep inside me.

When I sensed the temperature change, I paused, looking up at him.

Strain showed on his face. "Too cold?"

"It feels wonderful." I loved the heat of his cock, but now it felt almost as cold as the icicle—in a good way. A chill swept through me, but it only made me crave him more.

There must be people around, but not in the world we'd claimed as our own. Only the distant roar of the waves and the lone cry of a seagull broke through our gasps as we rocked closer and closer to ultimate pleasure.

He put everything he had into each thrust, his hand on my hip driving me down, the other stroking my clit.

Pressure built within me until I almost couldn't stand it. I tipped my head back and cried out as ripples started shooting through me, shocking their way to my fingertips and toes.

His cock tightened. It cooled and heated, flashing back and forth, and I sensed he was also losing control.

I could tell he was close, so I went faster, riding through my orgasm while pushing him nearer to his own.

"Mine," he growled. "All mine."

"I am," I whispered against his chest. "I'm claiming you, Elrik."

"Yes." He cupped the back of my head and tipped it back, his blue gaze blazing into mine.

Then he gave way, shuddering and jerking beneath me, falling into his own orgasm while groaning out my name.

28

ELRIK

As my cock warmed, I held her, stroking her back and whispering ancient words of love into her ear.

Finally, she shivered from the chilly night air, and I would not allow my mate to be cold even if I *was* an ice lord.

I slid her off my body and quickly fastened my pants. After lifting her underwear off the sand and stuffing it into my pocket, I grabbed my shirt and swept her up into my arms. I carried her back along the beach, passing the almost-melted ice sculpture, and up to the road. At the bench, I pushed my feet into my sandals, placing hers on her lap.

She smiled up at me, her face still suffused with the joy I'd given her. When she tucked her face against my chest, I only sighed and pulled her closer.

I strode down the sidewalk with pride blazing across my heart. This woman was mine and I was hers, and I wanted everyone in the world to know it. But I remembered how important it was not to attract attention, so I lowered her to her feet.

"I'll move my truck and come back to you." I stroked her hair away from her face. "Do you want to wait upstairs?"

"I'll wait right here."

With a grin splitting my face, I climbed into my truck and drove away, returning shortly after that on foot. After sweeping her off her feet again, I carried her up to her apartment and inside, kicking the door shut with my heel.

I placed her gently on her bed and stripped off her dress, then my own clothing.

Then I climbed over her and kissed her. Before the night was through, I planned to show her with my tongue and my cock that she was the only one I'd need for the rest of my life.

I WOKE the next morning to the buzz of my phone. Leaning over the edge of the bed, I snagged my shorts and pulled the device from the back pocket, scrolling into it when I saw it was a call from Katar.

"Hello?" I slid off the bed and padded from the room to keep from disturbing Melly who still slumbered. I'd kept her up most of the night, though I doubted she'd voice one complaint. I knew her well. She'd smile, curl her finger, and welcome me back to her bed.

"Hey, Elrik," Katar said. "I thought you might be in the office by now."

What time was it? A squint at the phone showed it was after nine. Wow. Okay. "I will be soon." This was the first time since taking this job that I would be late. Katar wasn't one to watch the clock since we'd often work all sorts of hours to complete a job, but he'd be within his right to chide me about lounging in bed until nine on a weekday.

"Someone's here to see you."

"Who?" Anyone related to this case? We'd made some progress, but I didn't feel much closer to exposing the person who'd framed Grannie Rose now than when I first started investigating.

"A woman," Katar said. "She didn't want to give her name."

"Tell her I'll be there shortly." I'd do my teeth here and wear my clothing from last night. I could go to my place and shower later.

"Awesome."

I ended the call and got ready in Melly's bathroom. Then I walked into the bedroom and stood beside the bed, grinning while I watched her sleep. There wasn't anyone lovelier than my Melly.

Since I didn't want to leave her with just a note, I climbed onto the bed and cupped her pretty face, kissing her deeply.

She moaned, and her arms went around my shoulders, stroking already. I'd give almost anything to be able to strip off my clothing and join her again beneath the covers, but I didn't want to keep the woman waiting. She could have important information related to the case, perhaps even details that would allow me to crack it. I looked forward to clearing Rose's name and then getting down on my knees and begging Melly to be my bride.

Would she say yes? I had to believe she would.

Rather than stroke her side and move my hand to her perky nipple, I lifted my head.

She gave me a sleepy smile. "Why are you dressed?" She plucked at my shirt. "Take this off. Get under the covers."

"I'd kill to do it, sweet, but someone's waiting for me at the office."

Her smile faded, and she frowned. "What time is it?"

"After nine."

"Ugh." She slid out from beneath me and out of the bed, bending forward to lift her robe off the floor, giving me the perfect view of her delectable ass and the gap between them.

I groaned.

She paused and peered at me over her shoulder. Smiling once more, she wiggled her ass. "Like the view?"

"You're killing me here."

Straightening, she tugged on her robe. "Take care of whatever you need to at the office and come visit me during your lunch break. We can sneak off somewhere for a quickie."

"I'm going to take you up on that offer." I sauntered around the bed, lifted her, and pressed her against the wall.

Her legs went around my chest, and she tugged me closer with the pressure of her heels. "Are you sure they can't wait?"

"It might be related to your case. I can't risk it. I won't

be long, though. What time do you have to be at Creature Cones?"

"Ten." With a sigh, she released me. "I miss you already."

I kissed her deeply, putting my heart and soul into my touch. When I lifted my head, she gave me a smile that melted everything still frozen inside me.

I stroked her face. "Soon."

"Soon," she said with a nod.

I drove out to the coffee place and waited in line before placing my order, then waited some more to pick my order up. Twenty minutes or so later, I parked my truck in the lot across from Monsters, PI. With a coffee and a bag holding a muffin in my hand, I jogged to the front door, opened it, and strode inside.

"There you are," Katar's wife, Bailey, said with a smile. "She's waiting in your office."

Oh, good. "This took longer than I thought it would." I held up my purchases.

"I'm sure she won't mind. We told her you weren't here but she said she was happy to wait."

"Great. Thank you." I walked past her and down the hall, waving to Katar sitting at his desk as I passed.

"Hey Elrik," Tuvid called out, and I stopped to poke my head into his open doorway.

"You're back," I said. "I hope you and Angie had an amazing honeymoon."

"The best." Tuvid grinned so wide, his face must hurt. "I wish we were still in Europe, but I guess we had to come back sometime."

"I imagine."

His smile fell. "Did Katar tell you someone's waiting in your office to speak with you?"

"Yup. I was just heading that way."

"Then I'll talk with you later."

With a wave, I continued to the last door on the right. The office opposite mine would soon be occupied with our newest hire, a dragon shifter detective. Another guy with wings like Tuvid who'd joked about being able to reach a job quicker than those of us who had to travel on foot or in a vehicle. Still, it would be cool to work with him. I bet he had some amazing stories to tell about his past job as a detective.

My office door was shut, but I opened it and strode inside.

My welcoming smile dropped fast.

"Brittney?" I snarled at my ex. "What are you doing here?"

29

MELLY

I brushed my teeth, took a shower, and dressed, then walked out to the kitchen on bare feet.

As I was taking eggs from the fridge to make an omelet, someone knocked on the door. I peeked around the curtain covering the window, seeing someone dressed in a blue uniform with a patch on her right chest stating *Griffon Express*, the name of Mystic Harbor's courier service. The griffon held a manilla envelope and a welcoming smile on her golden lion face.

I opened the door. "Hi."

"Melinda Brandt?"

"Yes."

She held out the envelope. "This is for you."

As I took it from her, I noted my name scrawled on the front. "Thank you."

"We aim to please." She clambered up onto the railing surrounding my small, second-story deck, and jumped off, her wings snapping out.

I watched in awe as she soared above Grannie's backyard and continued up over the building beyond.

Speaking of Grannie, I needed to go make her breakfast. She enjoyed sleeping in, and she never wanted more than tea first thing in the morning, but she'd soon be wondering where I was. I always checked in with her before I left for work.

I kicked the door shut and walked over to lay the envelope on my kitchen table. What could it be? I'd never received anything by courier before.

With a shrug, I unsealed the back and spread it open, peering inside.

Upending it, I slid a letter and an eight by ten photo out onto the table. I couldn't look away from the grainy image. The lighting was poor, but there was no mistaking me kneeling in front of Elrik, his cock buried deep within my mouth.

In a blur, I read the typed letter.

There's a garden behind Eerie Editions, the bookstore in the strip mall on the edge of town. In the back, beneath a tree, you'll find a wooden box. Leave ten thousand dollars in small bills inside by eleven this morning, and we won't take this and the rest of the pictures to your grandmother. We won't post them all over town. You wouldn't want to disappoint Grannie Rose with something like this, now would you?

Don't tell the cops. Don't bring your ice lord hero. And don't look around after placing the cash inside the box. Leave and don't look back.

We'll be watching. If you behave, so will we.

I snarled, flinging the letter on top of the photo.

Grannie would be upset if she saw pictures of me

pleasuring Elrik in this way. She'd be ashamed of me. The embarrassment would kill me, but that wasn't the worst thing about it.

If word of this spread through town, it would haunt us.

I'd spent most of my life hoping I wouldn't disappoint her.

This . . .

She'd be horrified if she saw something like this.

"I have to give them the cash," I whispered. "If I don't, I'll be ruined." I collapsed in a chair and cupped my face, sucking in a ragged breath before shoving it back out. Over and over until my head spun. I still couldn't figure out how I was going to get myself out of this situation.

"You're not alone," I said firmly, struggling to regain control.

Grabbing the letter and the picture, I stuffed them into the envelope and closed it once more.

I stopped in to see Grannie, who shooed me away, telling me she'd have a bowl of cereal later. She was in the middle of watching one of her favorite shows. She'd see me at dinnertime.

"Alright." I kissed her cheek and forced a smile.

She stared up at me, a frown appearing on her face. "What's wrong?"

"Nothing," I said, wishing my voice didn't come out shrill. "Nothing at all."

"Did you and Elrik fight?"

"Nothing like that. I . . . just need to go to the bank on my way to work, and I'm already running late."

She nodded slowly. "You'd tell me if there was a problem, right? You know I'm always here for you. I have been since before your mom died."

"I know that." I gave her a quick hug. "There's nothing wrong."

Nothing that couldn't be fixed.

I left and drove into town, parking in the lot across from Creature Cones. The bank was on my left at the end of the street.

It wouldn't take long to withdraw the money, though it would clean out all of my savings. That new equipment I'd been looking at online? I'd no longer be able to afford it. But there was enough to fix this, to make it go away.

Or not.

I sagged against my seat, tipping my head back to stare at the roof of my car.

More than likely, they'd demand more cash—money I didn't have. How long before I had to start thinking about selling my business?

I wasn't going to worry about that right now. No, I was going to take charge of this situation, and I knew how.

I left my car and strode into the small convenience store to the left of Boogey Beasts. After making a quick purchase, I hurried to Monsters, PI. I still had fifteen minutes before I had to deliver the cash and it would only take five to drive there.

I needed some reassurance, and there was only one person who could give it to me: Elrik.

"Hey, Melly," Bailey said.

"Is Elrik in his office?"

"He is. There's someone with him, but I imagine

they'll be finishing up soon. Would you like me to tell him you're here?"

"No, I'll just poke my head in and say hi. I need to get to work soon." If he was still busy, I could tell him everything later.

She nodded and gave me a smile before returning to her computer.

I walked down the hall, hearing people speaking inside the offices on my right, though the doors were closed, and I couldn't make out their words.

Elrik's door was cracked open, but I didn't hear anyone talking inside. Had he already left? Maybe he was on his way to see me.

I nudged open the door but came to a shuddering halt, my eyes widening as I took in the scene in front of me.

Elrik held a woman in his arms, and he was kissing her.

30

ELRIK

Just as Brittney lunged at me, I heard a sound at the door. As Brittney's lips landed on mine, I wrenched away from her.

Melly stood in the opening, gaping at us. Shock filled her eyes, followed by tears. As she spun around and fled from my office, I called out her name, but she didn't stop.

I knew what she was thinking. Her dad abandoned her when she was young. Her mom died, another abandonment. She wasn't confident anyone would ever truly be there for her.

She must think I'd blithely go back to Brittney if she curled her finger my way.

"Elrik," Brittney cried out, grabbing my arm as I tried to get past her. "Wait."

As Melly fled, I glared at Brittney. "What in the hell did you just do?"

She shook her head, and tears filled the eyes I'd adored from the time hormones first started surging through me. I'd seen her as a friend before that, but I suddenly felt awkward in my skin whenever she was around. I couldn't figure out what to do with my ungainly body, and my tongue was always tied in a knot.

"I made a mistake," she said. "I only want to be with you."

"Did my brother kick you out?"

Her face tightened, but her eyes gave her away. Her chin lifted. "The wedding's off."

"There won't be one with me. Go back to Canada. You won't find what you want here."

"You love me."

"I don't." After laying it out for her quickly, I rushed from my office and out onto the sidewalk, but I didn't see Melly anywhere.

Her car peeled out of the parking lot across the road and headed south on Main Street.

I rushed to my truck and took off after her. I had to catch up to her, had to tell her that I wasn't getting back with Brittney.

That I loved her.

I didn't want to run her off the road, however, so I followed at a slow pace, keeping far enough back she wouldn't realize I was there. When she stopped and got out, I'd beg her to let me explain.

She took the coastal road and pulled into the small strip mall on the edge of town. Since she was parking on the right side of the lot, I slowly passed the open area and pulled in on the opposite side, taking a spot far from her vehicle, beneath some trees with limbs extending out over the lot and among a cluster of other trucks to mask mine.

I got out, keeping low while I watched her leave her car. She held a white envelope. She didn't look my way, but I remained hunched down beside a black truck, peering over the hood. An ice lord had distinctive coloring, even in a town catering to monsters. Other than a few aliens, I was the only blue guy living in or around Mystic Harbor.

When Melly rounded the far end of the strip mall as if she was going to enter one of the buildings from a back entrance, I bolted after her, slinking to the end of the building and watching as she strode through the pretty garden behind Eerie Editions. I'd read about the place online. They encouraged guests to purchase a drink or snack from their small coffee shop inside and sit in the garden to savor their beverage while reading.

A wooden box had been placed beneath a broad oak tree on the far edge of the garden, close by the dense woods that stretched at least five or so acres toward the shore.

Melly stooped down in front of the box. After peering around, she opened it and placed the envelope inside. She straightened and backed away, pausing beside a bench to look every which way again.

I remained in the shadow of the building; confident she didn't see me.

There was no one around, not even inside the garden, though the bookstore didn't open until noon on weekdays.

With a frown, she walked back the way she'd come. I

waited, leaning against the building, letting the shade hide me.

She was walking past me when she came to an abrupt stop. Turning, she squinted toward me. “Elrik?”

“Can I explain?” I said.

31

MELLY

Leave it to an ice lord inspector to go incognito—or close to it.

"Did you follow me?" I asked in a shriller voice than I liked. I'd been swiping away furious tears since I saw him kissing a blue-skinned woman inside his office. By the time I'd reached the mini mall, I'd come up with a plan for both the blackmailer and him.

"I did."

Not even hiding it.

"I assume that's your ex."

I nodded.

"Lovely. Why bother to follow me? I'd think you'd be back in your office making plans with . . . with whatever her name is."

"Her name doesn't matter." He bumped off the side of the building and stalked right up to me, such a formidable presence that I stumbled backward. When I tripped over something, he grabbed my arm, holding me upright. He tugged me back into the shade of the building.

"What were you doing in the garden?" he asked in a deadly tone that might've intimidated a lesser woman. But a new Melly had stepped into wimpy Melly's shoes, and she wasn't having anything to do with a cheater.

I tugged away from him. "It's none of your business."

"I love you. Of course it's my business."

His words thrilled through me, and for a moment, I froze. "You don't love me. If you did, you wouldn't have kissed her."

"Brittney kissed me, not the other way around."

"That's the most clichéd thing I've ever heard." I lifted my voice, mimicking his. "Her lips were on mine. I couldn't stop it from happening. It meant nothing."

"It meant everything, because you seeing it caused you pain."

If I wasn't standing very close to him, I might not have heard his voice crack.

"She came here to get back together with me. She and my brother broke up. I told her no." He scratched the back of his neck, and his face darkened. "I told her I was in love with someone else, that I was going to beg her to marry me. I told her to turn around and go back to Canada because I didn't want her."

"You told her all that?" I said in a small voice.

"I did." His earnest gaze met mine. "You probably didn't know I was planning to propose." He patted his pocket. "I even have a ring here. I was going to wait a bit. We only started dating, and I didn't want you to feel rushed. But I planned to get down on one knee and ask you as soon as I thought you'd say yes."

"You bought a ring?" Stunned, I could only spit out one word. "Isn't that kind of sudden? We've only been seeing each other for . . . well, days."

"I love you. I have almost from the moment I met you." He swallowed. "I bought it yesterday. I didn't plan to spring it on you right away. I was going to take my time, work up to it. Give you a chance to know me completely before I begged you to be with me forever."

"You can't love me."

"I do." His soft smile rose, but it held sadness that speared right through me. "You're everything I could ever want. You're kind. Thoughtful. Generous. And you make me laugh. I love kissing you, touching you, and just being with you. I want to spend the rest of my life showing you how special you are, how much you mean to me."

This wasn't possible. "For so long, I've done all I could to please everyone else. I kept our apartment tidy to make my mom happy, though I doubted she noticed. She had to work two jobs to support us."

"You were a kid. It was her job to tidy the apartment, not the other way around."

I shrugged. "My mom knew where my dad was, so I wrote him long, cheery letters that I hoped would make him smile. I wanted him to realize what he was missing out on. I wanted him to know me. He never replied. For a while, I wondered if Mom somehow figured out I was writing to him and hid them. You know, like in those stories. The woman discovers her dad didn't get any of her letters, and when she hands them to him, he cries and hugs her." I sighed. "My dad didn't cry when he got them. When he died and they tracked me down because I was his next of kin and sole heir, I found the last letter I'd sent. He'd tossed it onto his cluttered dining room table, unopened. The rest weren't anywhere inside his apartment. I assume he threw them away."

"He didn't see the treasure he had in you."

Elrik needed to stop doing this, telling me I had worth when I wasn't sure I agreed.

"When Grannie Rose offered to finish raising me," I said. "I had to make sure she didn't regret it. I tried to remain quiet, to stay out of her way, to do everything I could to make sure she didn't reject me too."

"She loves you. You must see that."

I actually smiled. "I do. She does love me, and do you know what that means to me? I'll do anything I can to keep her from shoving me away."

"Anything."

"That's right." Tears streamed down my face. "That's why, when I got that nasty letter with the picture, I was very tempted to take all the money I'd saved from the bank and put it in an envelope, then leave it for the blackmailer."

"What?" he snarled, crouching while looking around as if a villain carrying a knife was racing toward us.

There was no one here, not yet. I could see the box from where I stood, though I doubted anyone waiting in the trees could see me since I was hidden in the shade of the building.

"Someone took pictures of us at the beach," I said. "Of me sucking your cock. They said they have others. I'm sure there's one of me riding you like a rodeo queen in a back alley behind a cowboy dive bar."

"Tell me what's going on."

I spilled it all out; there was no reason to hold it back. I'd bared myself to him, and the raw open wounds of my childhood still bled. But I'd planned to tell him about this when I saw him with his ex.

He cupped my face and tipped my head back, making my gaze meet his. What I saw there . . . It humbled me. Stunned me all over again. And it made me start crying.

"I adore you. I always will." His eyes sparkled with tears. "I hate what those who should've unconditionally loved you did to you. If I could, I'd go back and time and fix it for you. I'd take on your burdens. I'd hold your hand and tell you how wonderful you are. I'd make sure you knew right from the start that I'll love you every single day of our lives. I can't do that, but there's one thing I can do. I can share your burdens now. I can hold your hand and tell you that you're incredibly special. And I can tell you I love you the moment you wake up in the morning, plus a thousand times during the day."

He swallowed hard. "If you'll let me. I don't want to add another burden to those you already carry, so if you don't think you'll ever feel the same, if you don't want this from me, you need to tell me right now, and I'll back away. I'll still support you, but I'll do it from afar." Frowning, he cleared his throat. "Not in a stalkerish way either. Just as a friend. I want you happy and if being alone or without me in your life is what brings you joy, I'll support you in that too."

I couldn't breathe, but oh, how I could smile. "I want

all that, Elrik. I want you, because I'm in love with you too."

His mouth seared across mine in a kiss so sweet it made tears sting the backs of my eyes. He lifted his head too quickly. "I want to take you to my home or yours and love you all day long. I want to make you dinner and hold you. I want to sit on your little deck while the sun goes down. Walk along the shore, kicking at the waves, then take you to our bench again and shout out to the world that you're mine and that loving each other is nothing to be ashamed of."

A scowl chased away the joy on his face. "But first, we need to catch a blackmailer."

32

ELRIK

Melly loved me! I wanted to leap onto the top of the mini mall and bellow it out for the entire world to hear. I wanted to get down on one knee and offer her the ring I'd purchased for her. Ask her to make me the happiest ice lord in the world by consenting to be my bride.

But someone wanted to hurt her. That made me want to howl for a completely different reason.

And grind their face into the pavement before I called Detective Carter and told him to come arrest them.

"I didn't put money in the box, if that helps," Melly said, staring up at me with concern. She must've noticed my scowl. The gnashing of my teeth. The way I was clenching my hands into fists and aching to punch someone's nose.

"What did you put in the box?"

"Fake money I bought at the convenience store. The ten thousand dollars they asked for is all I have left of my inheritance. I'm not going to give it to someone because they took some pictures of me finding pleasure with the man I love."

My heart melted like an ice cube on a blazing hot day. My knees shook. I wanted to scoop her up and spin her around. Kiss her some more. Soon . . .

"I planned to hide in the bookstore and see who takes the box." She glanced in that direction. "It's still there, but they could be watching. We need to get out of view."

"I've got an idea." I whispered it to her.

She leaned away from me and smiled. "You're smart. I like that about you, Elrik."

"And here I thought it was my ability to produce cock-sized icicles."

"I think I prefer the real thing even more, but . . ." Her grin rose. "I might need another demonstration before I decide."

I definitely had to resist scooping her up and whirling her around.

"Wait for me," she said, staring at me with concern. "I won't be long."

I nodded, and she hurried to her car as planned, getting in and driving it out of the lot.

The blackmailer would see her leave. Did they see me in the shadows of the building? Also as planned, I went to my truck, starting it up and driving it out of the parking lot.

I pulled into the gas station across from the mall and left my vehicle. After crossing the street, I entered the woods and slowly made my way to a place where I could crouch among the bushes and watch the box from the forested side.

It remained in place, and I bet they hadn't hurried over to grab the money as soon as we left. They'd wait a while, watching to make sure we didn't return.

Movement to my left sent me spinning, but as expected, Melly crept close. A grin shone on her pretty face, and I knew why. The same heady, happy feeling was singing through my veins. We were together, and we were going to catch a blackmailer.

Was this related to the Xylitol poisoning? I hoped we'd find out.

Melly stooped down beside me and leaned against my arm. "Anything?" she asked softly.

I shook my head.

We watched. And waited.

And boy, were we surprised when we saw who left the bookstore and blithely strolled through the garden and over to the box.

33

MELLY

"Ginny?" I called out, straightening.

She jumped, and her gaze found us inside the woods. With the box under her arm, she spun and bolted for the bookstore.

Elrik flicked his finger and ice coated the walkway. She slipped and fell backward, landing hard on her ass and smacking her head on the ground.

While she lay on the melting ice, stunned, we walked over to stand on either side of her.

"Detective Carter's on the way," I said. I'd placed the call as I left the parking lot. Once I'd explained, he said he'd be right over. We weren't completely sure the blackmailer would show up right away, but he said he'd take the photo and letter as evidence.

"Why?" I asked as she sat up, rubbing her head and groaning.

"Why what?" she snarled.

"Why are you trying to blackmail me? I also assume you put Xylitol in the punch."

"I'm not admitting anything."

"I can see why blackmail might appeal, especially if it's lucrative. I'll be honest, though. I barely have ten thousand dollars to my name, so the well would've gone dry after one request."

"You have more. Grannie Rose told me how much you got from your dad."

"I *did* have more. When he died, I inherited the little he'd saved, plus his few possessions. I used most of the cash to open Creature Cones. I was saving the rest to upgrade equipment." I shook my head. "Did you put the Xylitol in the punch?"

She snarled.

"I can't understand why you'd want to ruin Grannie Rose," I said.

"I didn't want to ruin her." Ginny got to her feet and glared at us both. "I was trying to ruin you, Melly. Pretty, perfect Melly who could do no wrong. You always had things easy."

"What?" I couldn't believe what I was hearing.

"Grannie took you in. She raised you. She gave you everything you needed. She lets you have the apartment above the garage for practically nothing. She rented you the building on Main Street even after I offered her more for the chance."

"That's right. You wanted to open a coffee shop to compete with Mystic Mocha." It was so long ago; I'd forgotten about it.

"That building is the perfect location for a place like that. But, no, Grannie only wanted to rent to her precious granddaughter. Not me. Never me."

"You're my stepcousin, her sister's stepchild. She does care about you."

"Not since the divorce."

"Why did you want to ruin me?"

"Because then she'd see you for what you are, a leech, and she'd ditch you like she should've done when you were twelve."

"That's enough," Elrik snarled. "Melly has more worth in her pinky finger than you do in your entire body."

"Lay it all out for me," I said, noting out of the corner of my eye that Detective Carter was standing inside the woods, listening. "You put the Xylitol in the punch because you knew I'd made it while Grannie was recovering after fracturing her hip. You must've thought I'd made it that night as well."

"I didn't know *she'd* made it that evening," Ginny said. "You were supposed to. I wanted her to be angry with you for poisoning her friends."

"You dumped it in even though you knew it could hurt someone. Sue was hospitalized."

"She's fine."

"People were throwing up!"

She shrugged. "No one was seriously harmed."

"Then you cut Elrik's radiator lines and left that threatening note."

"Which should've made you stop looking into this," she said.

"I couldn't let my grandmother go to jail," I snarled. "Then you review-bombed Creature Cones."

"That should've ruined you too. You should be crying

while closing your ice cream shop, begging someone to step in and buy your used equipment, which I would've done at a fraction of the cost. I would've sold it for a nice profit."

"You suck," I huffed.

"If you'd let this go," she said, "I wouldn't have taken pictures of you and Elrik at the beach. I wouldn't have needed money to give myself a new start."

"No more plans for a coffee shop?" Elrik asked.

"I want to leave town."

"But you're taking care of Bob," I said.

"And you're practically running Sterling Life and Indemnity," Elrik added.

"Bob's shoving me out as if I haven't spent all this time not only ferrying him around from one engagement to another but keeping that business afloat. I was the one who talked Grannie Rose into backing away from a lawsuit after she fell. I sold more policies over the past year than he did in the two prior years combined."

"What else have you done?" I asked, feeling incredibly defeated. I hadn't been close to Ginny while growing up; she was older than me. But I thought we respected each other, if nothing else. Now I felt like I'd cared for a stranger.

"Remember a few weeks ago when people started complaining that your ice cream tasted like pickles and black pepper?" she said with a sneer.

I sputtered. "You sabotaged my ice cream?"

"If you hadn't dumped it out, you would've earned those one-star reviews," she said.

All I could do was shake my head and back away as Detective Carter strode forward.

"Will you come with me peacefully, or do I need to put you in cuffs?" he asked. His nod took in me and Elrik, and I knew he'd take it from here. Ginny would be arrested and charged. Grannie Rose's name would be cleared. And we'd all try to move on from this betrayal.

She shot me a glare before nodding to him. "Don't cuff me."

Detective Carter led Ginny away. She kept shouting about how she was still going to ruin me, how she was going to show the pictures to Grannie, how she was going to tack copies on the bulletin board in town hall.

She'd soon realize that this was over, that she no longer held any power over me or Grannie Rose.

Elrik held out his arms, and I leaped into them. He held me while I struggled to gain control of my turbulent emotions.

"I'll tell Grannie," I whispered against his neck. "I won't show her the picture Ginny sent, but I'll tell her about it and let her know there are others. If she rejects me, then that's how it goes."

"I don't think she will." He stared down at me with so much love in his eyes that no matter what, I knew everything was going to be alright. "No one respects a blackmailer, but everyone adores you."

"I have enough saved to weather any storm Ginny might send my way."

"*We* have the strength to weather whatever storm someone chooses to send *our* way."

For the first time since I opened the envelope, I felt complete joy in my heart. "You're right. I'm not alone any longer. I have you in my life and in my heart."

"Always."

And then he kissed me.

34

EPILOGUE

MELLY

"I need help." A woman with dark hair in a blunt cut with bangs and streaked with auburn said from the entrance to Monsters, PI. "My B&B is haunted," she said in a rush over to the front desk where I was filling in for the day.

Bailey had needed time off, and I'd volunteered. It was the least I could do. Carla did so well with our PR disaster at Creature Cones that I'd promoted her to a managerial position and hired someone new to take her place at the counter. She'd confessed about her financial situation and told me the raise was welcome.

I pushed again for her to hang some of her art in the shop, and she reluctantly agreed. To her surprise, it was selling—at a very high price.

The realtor had found buyers for her place in Florida and here in Mystic Harbor, and she'd not only make enough to pay off all the bills, but she'd also have enough to put some in the bank and make a deposit on a small condo in town. She confessed she was looking forward to putting her past behind her and savoring her new life.

"I'm sorry." Frowning at the woman who'd just entered Monsters, PI, I stood and walked around the reception desk. "But did you say your B&B is haunted?"

"Let me back up a sec." She flashed me a smile. Pretty, she was tiny and slender, and her dark eyes contrasted nicely with her pale skin. "I'm Hannah Everett. I bought the old Blakemore place."

"The one where Justin Blakemore died?" I winced. Maybe I shouldn't have brought that up. But that was what I'd heard around town. He'd died of old age, but still, some might consider a thing like that creepy.

She huffed but softened it with a sweet smile. "That was six years ago. The building has been vacant since. It was tied up in probate. The heirs sold it to me a short time ago." Her smile grew. "I'm fixing it up, and let me tell you, it needs a ton of work. But I'm strong." She lifted her arm and flexed the muscles. "My dad taught me how to do almost any kind of construction myself. My plan is to open in the next few months but I'm floundering. I swear, the place is haunted. I think Justin is trying to keep me from opening it as a B&B."

"Why do you think Justin's doing anything? Ghosts don't exist."

She shrugged. "So says someone who's marrying an ice lord."

"Me," Elrik said, striding down the hall to join us. He crossed the foyer and went around to stand at my back, wrapping his arms around me. "She's marrying *me*." He kissed my cheek. "In two months' time."

We would hold the wedding on the beach near where we'd sat and enjoyed our icy treats. Even his family was coming. His brother and once-again fiancée had opted not to join us, but I hadn't complained about that. I wanted my wedding day to be perfect. Smiling and making nice with the woman who'd cheated on Elrik with his brother was nowhere close to perfect. We'd only invited them to be polite.

When Grannie Rose found out what Ginny had done, she'd stormed to the courthouse and snarled at her step-niece. Then she'd hugged me and told me that she loved me, that no one could ever steal that emotion away. She said she didn't care about any old photos. She did tap my arm and tell me to take more care with where I loved my fiancé—following it up with a wink.

During the investigation, I'd discovered a side to my Grannie I'd never seen before, and I loved this grandmother as much as the one I already knew.

As for Bob, he was selling Sterling, and he'd hired a new caregiver, a yeti who Bob said was doing an amazing job.

I'd finally come to terms with my past, and while it had shaped me into who I was today, I wasn't going to let it mold me into someone full of sadness, not when I deserved only joy. This was the hardest lesson of all: accepting that I was worthy. But within the shelter of Elrik's love, I was making strides.

I realized I loved myself, and that was the best thing of all.

"Naturally, I don't believe in ghosts," Hannah said. "So I need someone to help me figure out what's going on at my soon-to-open B&B. Someone is sabotaging me, and I can't let it continue. That's why I came here. Detective Carter was kind enough to look around, but he couldn't find evidence that anyone was doing something criminal. He suggested I come here."

"We'll be glad to help you." Elrik slid my hair to the side and kissed the back of my neck. My legs quaked, and it was all I could do not to swoon back in his arms.

"I'm working, sweetie," I said, sure he could hear the tremor of desire in my voice.

"I suppose I should get back to work as well." He stepped away from me, which allowed me to regain control of my brain long enough to think.

"This sounds like a great job for Reylor," I said. Katar had hired the former detective dragon shifter not long ago, and Reylor had recently finished his orientation. He was eager to take on his first case.

"Let me go grab him," Elrik said. When he strode down the hall, I stared after him, trying not to sigh.

"He's cute," Hannah said politely. "I've met all sorts of monsters since I moved to Mystic Harbor, but I hadn't yet met our resident ice lord. He's not as chilly as I'd expected."

"He can be abrupt at times, but he's warm and squishy beneath his icy demeanor."

She nodded. As she stared down the hall, her eyes widened.

Elrik joined us with Reylor.

Reylor had gorgeous dark auburn hair, lots of muscles, and he could shift into a dragon. What could be better than that?

My ice lord, but truly, a dragon shifter was amazing.

He was handsome from his golden scales to his tight ass—something I hadn't really, truly, actually noticed. Not too much. I was so in love with Elrik, it was a wonder I could see anyone else long enough to keep from bumping into them.

"What can I do for you?" Reylor drawled, his attention completely on Hannah.

Hannah kept making little gasping sounds, and her dark eyes only widened. "You're . . ." She swallowed hard.

"Reylor Crandish, one of the staff detectives." His hand jutted out.

He had the sexiest drawl, almost as appealing as Elrik's.

Hannah took his hand and for a second, she slumped. I worried she was going to pass out, but she stiffened her spine and blinked her long lashes up at Reylor. "I'm Hannah Everett. I'm in dire need of your help."

Reylor nodded solemnly. "Why don't you come to my office, sweetheart, where you can explain."

"Yes. Office. Explain," Hannah said in a limp voice. "Don't call me sweetheart. It's patronizing."

"Only if I don't mean it."

She blinked up at him. "*Do* you mean it?"

His smile widened. "Let's go talk in my office." He led her down the hall and shut the door behind them.

"Funny how that keeps happening," Elrik said with a grin.

"What?" I sauntered over to him and I traced my fingertip down the front of his button-up shirt.

"Every one of us has fallen hard for someone who came to Monsters, PI for our services."

"Maybe because your services are superior to all others." I snickered.

His grin widened, and he tugged me into his arms. "I was about to take my lunch break. Why don't we . . ." Leaning close, he whispered by my ear. "We could take a long walk on the beach. Visit our favorite bench."

"Let's save that for after it gets dark." Per Grannie's hint, we'd been more careful, but there was something freeing about being with the man I loved out in the open. We took every opportunity we could find to explore that facet of our personalities. "However, we could go to my apartment. Bailey should be here soon to cover for me."

"I'm here now." Bailey strode through the front door and walked over to us, noting our clasped hands. "When you come back, you can cover for me and Katar." She rested her hand on her big belly. Their child would be born soon, and I couldn't wait to hold it. Kiss it. "We have a lunch date."

"Of course," I said.

"Then take off, you two." Her eyes sparkling with humor, Bailey flicked her hand toward the door. "Take your time."

Elrik and I just grinned at each other.

We left the building and crossed Main Street to the parking lot. Inside his truck, I buckled while he strode around to climb into the driver's seat.

"What would you think of having a child one day?" he asked as he pulled his truck out onto Main Street.

"I think it would be amazing. Someday."

"Someday." With a sweet smile, he reached across and took my hand, squeezing it. "That's you, my precious love. Amazing. Just want to make sure you know that."

"I love you, Elrik."

He kissed me. "Love you too."

I hope you enjoyed Elrik & Melly's story!
I'm having so much fun with my cozy monster mystery romances, and I can't wait to share the next story in the series, Detective Dragon.
Can Reylor get to the bottom
of the B&B ghost mystery,
and will he and Hannah fall in love?

You can find Ava's books on Amazon
& on her website, avarosswrites(dot)com.

DETECTIVE DRAGON

Do I dare trust my heart to Detective Dragon?

Hannah: The building I'm renovating to turn into a B&B in the cozy coastal town of Mystic Harbor, where humans and monsters live in harmony, is either haunted or someone's trying to sabotage me.

After someone rips up my flower beds for the third time, and the local law enforcement can't find any clues, I head to Monsters, PI, where I hire a much-too-gorgeous dragon shifter to determine if I'm a victim of crime or paranormal activity. After someone creeps through my building late at night, Reylor moves in with me to further his investigation. Now that I'm bumping into him in the kitchen and snuggling up with him on the sofa, is it my fault if I'm falling in love?

Reylor: I don't believe in ghosts, though I do believe that whoever's sabotaging Hannah's building renovations needs to be locked up for good. From the moment I meet Hannah, I know she's my fated mate. I'll do everything to protect her and solve this crime. If that means moving in with her and watching over her twenty-four-seven, then I'm the right detective for the job.

And when the case is closed? I'm going to make Hannah mine.

Detective Dragon is Book 3 in the Monsters, PI Series. It's a cute and steamy romance featuring a cinnamon roll dragon shifter, on-the-page heat, a cozy mystery, humor, and a HEA guaranteed.

Other Books in the Series:
Undercover Orc (part of Sweet Monster Treats)
Secret Agent Gargoyle
Ice Lord Incognito
Dragon Detective
Top Secret Vampire
Ogre on Patrol

ABOUT THE AUTHOR

Ava Ross is a two-time *USA Today* Bestselling author who has written numerous titles, all of them featuring sweet and steamy romance. She fell for men with unusual features when she first watched Star Wars, where alien creatures have gone mainstream. She lives in New England with her husband (who is sadly not an alien, though he is still cute in his own way), her kids, and a few assorted pets.

avarosswrites(dot)com

Printed by Libri Plureos GmbH in Hamburg,
Germany